I0631451

Christopher L. Pindar

Alleghania

Praises of American Heroes

Christopher L. Pindar

Alleghania
Praises of American Heroes

ISBN/EAN: 9783337194338

Printed in Europe, USA, Canada, Australia, Japan

Cover: Foto ©Andreas Hilbeck / pixelio.de

More available books at **www.hansebooks.com**

OR,

PRAISES OF AMERICAN HEROES.

BY

CHRISTOPHER LAOMEDON PINDAR.

PHILADELPHIA:

J. B. LIPPINCOTT & CO.

1868.

TO

MY FELLOW-CITIZENS

OF THE

AMERICAN REPUBLIC.

THOUGH young and little skilled in the goodly
craft of poesy, I feel an unusual confidence in
offering this tiny volume to your kind regard.
My ground of assurance lies in this. When a
good child has been sadly bereaved of a noble
father, nothing delights it more than to hear a
tender word spoken in his praise. However
simple be the deed, how uncouth soever the
terms in which it is lauded, these demand but
little attention of the infant heart. The parent
of its love is praised; this is enough; the most
brilliant epic of foreign and bygone heroes vanishes before that simple tale. In the simplicity
of my heart I have compared the people of our

glorious Union to such a child, the war-worn
patriots of her dawning Independence to such a
father, and my own little self to such an artless
narrator.   Having formed this comparison, it
can no longer seem strange that I feel confident
of my task; should I fail unfortunately, it is
surely not owing to the want of a good heart;
this I bring with all its tender springs to a sub-
ject so long the darling dream of my boyhood.

But while the like quaint reasoning inspires
me to brave with courage the roaring surges of
remorseless criticism, I cannot help feeling the
sad conviction that it is the only rudder left me
to keep my clumsy little ship afloat.   Nay, what
is most of all disheartening, I already perceive
some prowling pirate of letters trying to sink me
at the very outset.   On his blood-red flag I read
these startling words: "What an Irving and a
Bancroft have narrated in brilliant prose, what
a Bryant and a Halleck have sung in melodious
verse, what even a Byron has immortalized in
many a glowing rhyme—too daring stripling,'
forbear to pollute!"   Fortunately or unfortunately, however, I have been gifted by Nature
with a peculiar attribute.   The more I am op-

posed, the bolder and more determined I become. Were it not for the bitter remarks bestowed on some of my earlier verses, I should probably have never written another line. But out of pure spite for these unsparing grandees I felt it a most agreeable labor to continue cultivating the Muses; impelled no less, however, by the parental encomiums given to me so kindly by learned man and loving woman. Never shall I forget their heartfelt benevolence to a struggling youth.

To comprise now in a few words the two principal aims I had in writing the following poem: the first was, that I might prove my gratitude for those immortal heroes whose blood procured for me and million others a country than which for liberal institution and enlightened enterprise no better can be found on earth; the second, that I might contribute a little with my slender abilities to keep alive the spark of patriotism in my fellow-citizens, well aware that only this can uphold the stately fabric of Freedom upreared by the labor of so many valorous hands, and moistened with the sweat and blood of the purest patriots that ever drew the sword. If I succeed in these my wishes to only a limited extent, I shall not regret the few solitary hours devoted to my task. But if, in addition, some of you, my dearest countrymen, should in perusing these pages find your bosoms heave with the love of Liberty, if some of you, illustrious matrons, should in reading the praises of our forefathers perceive your hearts turned to the mouldering corpse of the darling son, whose blood still reddens the recent battle-fields for the cause of Union, and thinking of him feel the motherly tear drop from your affectionate eyes,—the tear not so much of sorrow as of joy that you had a son worthy of his father,—oh then! I wish no more; my tears shall mingle with yours, as often they have done before; my heart shall say to me: America cannot be lost while such are her daughters and such her patriot sons!

C. L. P.

CONTENTS.

(ix)

ALLEGHANIA.

CANTO I.

HESPERIA'S sons against Britannia's king
For Freedom battling, Alleghania, sing !
That race divine, whose fearless lips denied
Oppression's tribute, and whose arms defied
Her mighty legions wafted o'er the main
From Europe's realms to spread tyrannic reign.
Long raged the conflict, wars succeeding wars,
Ere Freedom basked beneath her thirteen stars;
And thrived, sustained by heavenly decree,
The Great Republic, home of brave and free.
   Thee, Alleghania, progeny divine,
New-fated sister of the sacred Nine !
Ordained by Heaven athwart Hesperian climes
To waft the symphony of dulcet rhymes,
The magic numbers of the Grecian lute
To blend with weird notes of the Indian flute,—

My theme demands.   To gain thy gentle lore
Up to thy mountain home I fleetly soar;
Where Appalachus wrapt in clouds distils
Celestial dews, that float in silver rills
This way and that, thence through the valleys gleam
Far in Ohio's or Potomac's stream.
Thine eyes, oh Muse!   have from this cliff reviewed
Each stern debate, each field with gore imbrued,
Th' embattled hills enwrapped in death's eclipse,
Old ocean heaving with rebellowing ships;—
Thou knowest all!   Now take me to thy side,
And in my pathless wanderings me guide!
The theme so grand, unless a Goddess aid,
I wander lonely and sink down dismayed;
But thou with me, a sacred rapture fires
My youthful breast, and heavenly thoughts inspires.
  She smiles assent.   Far from her cloud-capt height,
O'er hills and vales in spring arrayed, our flight
We swiftly urge to that delightsome land
Whose rocky shore first hailed the Pilgrim band,
When to escape Oppression's fierce decrees
They sought a home beyond Atlantic seas;
Whence sprung the race in Liberty's bright van
E'er battling for the equal rights of man.
First in the cause, which made Hesperia free,
The Bay State arms her sturdy yeomanry

Against th' inhuman despot who opposed
Her freeborn trade and all her commerce closed.
Fierce lours his vengeance on the fearless band
Who durst resist his insolent demand.
Arms clashing wild the longlived stillness break
With doomful din, and swale and hillock shake.
Along the beach with thunders opened wide
Huge ships of war plough through the rumbling tide,
Intent to sweep in blood away the stain
Of baneful cargoes hurled into the main.
Already brought is Freedom's sacrifice
On Lexington's first-hallowed green, where lies
The gallant Parker with the patriot seven
Alive though dead, on earth though raised to heaven.
For, like the seed which dying lives anew
In plant and tree, from out their corses grew
That stem of heroes gathering on their graves
The sacred valor of Hesperian braves.
Nor slow the growth, but in the selfsame day
At Concord fructified the godlike bay;
Where twoscore hearts, by dauntless Davis led
Against the foe, with chief devoted bled;
Yet not till seventy British slain had swelled
The gory heap, the rest been all repelled;
In headlong terror to the shore they dashed,
And first my country's star of Freedom flashed.

2

But fierce Bellona now Dissension's fires
Shoots from her breast, and all the war inspires.
From Albion's isle distressful moanings ring,
Whole legions crowd to battle for their king.
As when the lion suddenly is roused
From out the lair where coseyly he drowsed,
The rush of huntsmen first distracts his brain,
And for awhile he sourly seeks the plain,
Then all at once his haughty self returns,
And madly roaring on his foes he turns:
So Britain felt the smart of slighted pride,
And sprang with fury to the war untied.

Hesperia sees the raging storm arise,
With clouds of thunder filled the quivering skies;
Yet triumph won may laurels new deserve,
And hope uplifted strengthens every nerve.
Thus on Nebraska's vast and reeded plain
The wounded bison shakes his shaggy mane,
When victim to an ill-dissembled scorn
The reckless Pawnee bleeds beneath his horn;
Flushed with his triumph he anew prepares
His awful front and all the red host dares.
Not less America, with hope inspired,
Her eager warriors to the combat fired.

O'er Boston's walls a lofty hill uprears
His rounded brow, that like a tower appears

In solemn grandeur and terrific state
Decreed to guard the bay's and city's fate.
There, while dark silence reigned o'er sea and land,
The wary Prescott ranged his trusty band ;
From sea to river with a frowning mound
Of earth and iron all the summit crowned.
Day streaked the east, and ushered into light
The work herculean of the laboring night,
The foe above in doom impending flashed
On foe below with sudden fear abashed,
Those perched like eagles in aerial nest,
These like sea-cormorants on the beach compressed.
Fear, shame commingled rend the Briton host,
To shield themselves sinks their defiant boast,
And stung with rage their thousands throng the
    coast.
  Gage thunders o'er the town his stern commands,
And Howe and Pigot arm their martial bands.
In marshalled ranks three thousand warriors shine,
Gun siding gun, and line uprolling line.
As when against a mountain's craggy side
Swelled by the storm sweeps on the furious tide,
Each new-formed wave the wave before impels,
Till high upon the rock the torrent swells :
So moved Britannia's ranks 'mid trumpet's shrill
In dreadful order up th' embattled hill :

While charged with thunder fast her ships of line
Along the beach cleaved through the rushing brine;
Then facing round from mouths distended wide
With flaming meteors smote the mountain's side.
Sulphureous clouds hang quivering between,
As if to veil the horrors of the scene.

High from their mount, impatient for the fray,
The bold Hesperians all this storm survey.
Though one to two, each bosom Freedom warms
With ardor doubled, and with power arms.
Nor kindly Powers withheld the hand of Fate
The fortune threading of a lovèd State;
E'en vied to rouse from peaceful walks of life
The latent warrior to the coming strife.
At, Pallas, thine and Liberty's command
The youthful Warren joins the leaguered band;
Skilled both to heal with Esculapian art,
And soothe the sorrows of his country's heart;
Alike to pen the patriotic word,
And on the battle-field to wield the sword.
Not unprepared he rushes on the foe,
Unlaurelled not his fiery temples glow;
That beauteous lock my eyes behold no more—
I look around, and see it steeped in gore;
Where late at Cambridge desperate in the fight
He hung in terror on the Briton's flight.

Now ring again his country's dire alarms,
Again he lists, and thunders in his arms.

  When love of country fires the breast of man
He asks no honor but the glorious van;
The first to listen to her piteous call,
So first in battle for her cause to fall;
He scorns the gewgaw of supreme command,
His highest joy in danger's front to stand.
On Freedom's battle-ground contentions cease
(That bane of nations or in war or peace).
Here valor reigns supreme, and o'er the brave
No honors but his country's banners wave;
His sole contention for the dreaded front,
His sole delight to bear the battle's brunt.

  Thus on the heights of Bunker Hill awhile
Sweet virtue lingered with her heavenly smile.
Th' impetuous Warren thundering to the storm,
"Where, where's the danger? where can serve my
      arm?"
Him noble Prescott from the rampart eyed,
He leaps adown and hastens to his side:
"Come, valorous warrior, thine the chief command,
Mine to obey, and by thy side to stand!"
"No!" cried the youth; "a skilless sword is mine,
To rule the storm of war thy art divine.

I came not hither to urge on the brave,
But urged by them my country's rights to save.
Give me the rampire most by danger pressed,
A living buttress will I give my breast!"

He said; and rushing to the clouded mound
The brother-patriots ranged their men around;
Yet curbed their spirit, and refrained to throw
At once their thunders on the nearing foe.
In measured terror surged the dreadful van
Of Albion's host, close-banded man to man;
On nearer, nearer, till scarce thirty ells
From facing horrors fraughtful space repels.
" Fire !" Prescott cries; and with terrific roar
Full thousand guns their volleyed meteors pour.
Clap follows clap; in horrid concord flies
The quivering flash, the sulphurous clouds uprise;
Triumphant shouts from Bunker's forehead peal,
Distressful groans rebounds his bloody heel.
Five hundred Britons welter in their gore,
The rest bound headlong to the saving shore.

Gage eyed the havoc with distorted mien,
And bit his lips in fury at the scene;
Again he roared his insolent command,
To face the terrors of the conquering band.
Shame and revenge the British bosoms fill,
Renewed they storm upon th' embattled hill.

Hesperia's braves with courage quickened glow,
Again they hurl their deadly showers below.
Once more five hundred burst the living vein,
Confusion stalks in terror o'er the plain.
But now the genius of Britannia rears
Her wonted bulwarks, and her warriors cheers.
Repelled with tumult from the foreign steep,
She plants her hope upon her native deep.
Thus when the redman on the open plain
Against the whites' close legions wars in vain,
He slily slinks into the bushy glen,
There lording like a lion in his den.
Such skilful power Albion's art displays,
With conscious pride her ocean might she sways,
And 'neath her waves the mountain rampire lays.
Say, Alleghania, why should tyrant power
Force but a moment Freedom's knee to cower?
When Liberty Oppression's host repelled,
Why o'er her sway at once her funeral knelled?
Ye Gods, that rule unfeeling Fates above,
Shall despots more than patriots win your love?
"Oh, mortal rash!" the heavenly Muse replies;
"Unfathomed Wisdom flees terrestrial eyes.
Awhile her judgments cruel to you seem,
Your dearest hopes are scattered like a dream;

But eft returns Truth's undisputed reign—
Lie's shortlived triumph never can remain."

　Sulphureous mists veil all the scene below,
My tearfilled eyes scarce ken or friend or foe.
Unpitying flashes rend the pulverous veil,
Revealing Glasgow's guns and Lively's sail,
With Falcon's batteries in terror lined,
And toward the mount with showery death inclined
From war-filled Boston Clinton heads his band
Of vigorous soldiers to the bloody strand.
Surviving braves their beaten ranks reform,
And all with courage to the combat storm.

　With presage hopeless our Hesperians view
The shock of hosts against a shattered few;
Yet valor's ardor every bosom fires,
And love of country every heart inspires.
High from the mound they hear their captain's call:
"Freedom or death! die on or save the wall!"
His towering form above them all appears,
His hand them guides, his word their courage cheers.
Like lions roused to rage, they fiercely throw
Their breasts devoted on the thundering foe.
Destructive might must conquer, but its blaze
Can only trophies to the vanquished raise.
They fall, but forward with their breasts opposed,
And guns still clinched on towering slain imposed.

In monumental glory, saved to last,
The zealous Warren sinks beneath the blast.
His arm still rises in destroying power,
When round him pours the foe's death-darting shower;
Their murderous balls transpierce his lordly brain,
He staggers, droops, and joins his comrades slain.
Thus falls the lion on his whelps and mate,
The first to brave, the last to share their fate.
Unfearèd death ennobles all defeat,
The patriot's grave excels the victor's feat.
Hesperia's children fondly lift their eyes
To Bunker's summit as to Freedom's rise.
His gallant dead soar to immortal fame,
And every tongue speaks proudly Warren's name.

CANTO II.

In marble sheen adorned with sylvan lines
The city of fraternal love reclines.
Pure is her bed, preserved from gore of men
By peaceful arts, the gift of gentle Penn.
No fears of savage war her bosom rend,
The Quaker's hand makes every foe a friend.
With arms no other than to till the soil,
She fosters charms no jealousy can foil,
And rises fairest of all cities fair
Atween clear Schuylkill and broad Delaware.
    Such godlike city, Freedom, it became
To echo first the triumph of thy name.
Such gentle walls should be designed by Fate
To hear thy champions mighty in debate.
Here Heaven decreed should ring the potent word
Of Independence to direct the sword.
    Tell me, my Muse, what sapient men the cause
Of Freedom strengthened with celestial laws!
Who hither sent from thirteen colonies
Here framed the noblest of all earth's decrees?

From Massachusetts came her Adams twain
With fearless Hancock and judicious Paine.
Virginia sent her Wythe and Harrison
With fiery Lee and thoughtful Jefferson.
From Penn's woods Dickinson (a dolorous name!),
Wilson and Morton and great Franklin came;
Him Pallas armed with her mysterious rod
To break the thunders of th' Olympian God.
Ontario's sons consigned the doubtful day
To Clinton, Livingston, and youthful Jay.
Bartlett and Whipple guarded Hampshire's fate,
Hopkins and Ellery the Island State.
Her sister, learned liberty to save,
Sherman and Huntington to Freedom gave.
An equal fame Mackean and Rodney share,
Who guard the fate of little Delaware.
From Jersey Witherspoon the pious came,
And Hopkinson crowned with poetic fame.
Fair Maryland eternal glory won
In Paca, Chase, and him of Carrollton.
Gwinnett and Hall came from Savannah's plain
With those whom sent the Carolinas twain:
Hooper and Hewes she with the golden hair,
Rutledge and Middleton the dark-eyed fair.

In that grand dome, as Independence Hall
Thence known to future age, they gather all.

With concord feelings beat their bosoms brave,
One lofty thought lined every forehead grave.
Each felt the fortunes of his native land
For weal or woe entrusted to his hand.
High o'er them all the outlawed Hancock sate,
His care to rule and perfect the debate.
Loud throbbed each bosom; when Virginia's son,
The ardent Lee, arose and thus begun:
　" Oh noble patriots, whose undaunted arms
Have leaped in terror to your land's alarms,
Beneath whose strokes has sunk the tyrant's host
On Bunker's Hill and Carolina's coast,
Whose sons and brothers Freedom's van have led
To laurelled combat, and for her have bled—
Shall all this blood have been effused in vain,
Shall still we cower to the despot's rein?
Where lives the cause that drew the vengeful blade,
Where rings the call that thousand hearts obeyed?
Ancestral rights derided were the cause,
Th' alarm was pealed for independent laws.
Why then not carry out the brave design,
And fearlessly uprear the patriot sign?
If not, the shame and vengeance of the world
Shall on our valor in contempt be hurled;
And where we might the patriot's laurels gain,
As lawless rebels we shall reap disdain.

Hence I opine, and thinking speak my mind:
No tie shall more our land to Albion bind;
Not more allegiance shall our arms her own
Than Swiss unfettered bring to Austria's throne;
And, as is just, these Federal Colonies
Shall own no power but their own decrees."

Thus spoke the bravest of the Leean race,
Men trained in arms, and skilful in the chase.
Quick as he said, applauding cries rebound
The vaulted roof and every word resound.
One only silent sat the crowd among,
The timid Dickinson. Smooth was his tongue,
Trained to the schools, and studious of each word,
Each thought ere spoken twice had been deferred;
A tardy politician, loath to draw
Conclusions rash from theoretic law.
He loved his country, but preferred to give
Purse more than blood, and so contented live.
When ceased the shout, he beckoned with his head,
And standing up his cautious mind he said:

"With joy, my brethren, should I hail the day
When Freedom's wand would o'er my country sway.
None more than I can love his natal soil,
None from her chains with greater dread recoil.
I prize the bold Virginian's heartfelt zeal;
Sylvania's sons an equal ardor feel.

3

Yet while for trampled rights my bosom glows,
I fear to change them into greater woes.
Well know ye all Britannia's far-famed power,
How seas and empires 'neath her lion cower.
Should we, scarce born to life, presume to wage
Imprudent wars against such potent rage,
What other than the reckless rebel's meed,
Ignoble death, should be o'er us decreed?
To such result, I pray, in time attend,
Ere fall disasters none can then amend."

He ceased; a murmur of displeasure rose,
As on the beach the adverse current flows.
Fired at the insult, Massachusetts' son,
Adams of Braintree, ardently begun:

"How long shall Diffidence her puny hand
Lend to the despot, and enslave our land?
How long shall courtiers nibble at the tower
Of Liberty upreared by valor's power?
Just is our cause, no brave man e'er gainsaid,
Or vainly else six hundred hearts have bled.
Strength, such as patriot breasts is wont to fill,
Rests in our arms.   Look up to Bunker Hill!
Or, that I may not seem my own to boast,
Direct your eyes to Carolina's coast!
Where scarce six days ago three hundred braves
Britannia's bulwarks scattered o'er the waves.

Closed in their humble fort they calmly viewed
Her surging citadels with thunders brewed.
'Mark every shot!' the simple Moultrie said;
'The powder's scarce; for every ball a dead.'
And sitting down he smoked his little pipe
(Thus fears our eagle for the lion's gripe).
On Bristol sailed with fifty thunders bent,
And Active swift and huge Experiment.
Their guns lie levelled; straight the volleyed balls
Fly, but repelled by soft palmetto walls.
Then peals the answer from our brazen lips,
And groaning quake the bosom-shivered ships.
Peal follows peal.   Hesperia's scanty fire
Fanned by the Powers uprears Britannia's pyre.
When lo! a ball with matchless fury swayed
Rushed high in air and low our flagstaff laid.
But quick as thought the gallant Jasper leapt
Unto the beach, and, while around him swept
Incessant showers of flaming balls, unfeared
Snatched up the flag, upon a halberd reared
The tattered glory, up the merlon flew,
And proudly waved it toward the gnashing crew.
Bellona flapped her wing, the flash relumed,
Blew pallid death, while shots incessant boomed
Athwart the trembling wave, to many a breast
Swelled with tumultuous hope a chilly rest.

Thus wore the day, till even's sombre fall
Spread o'er the watery grave her funeral pall.
Swift Active lay a wreck, proud Bristol rent
With gaping chinks, and huge Experiment
Struck low with shattered sails, and all the line
Disordered fled across the saving brine.
O'er Moultrie's Fort our flag triumphant waved,
The South respired, her Ocean Queen was saved."
   Unisonant applause here fills the hall;
No more debate; for Freedom's chart they call.
Their valorous titles glitter on the page
Defiance hurling to the tyrant's rage.
The listening bells the strains harmonious seize
And waft them gaily on the quavering breeze.
From every dome, from every cottage pour
The swelling crowds, and storm the Senate door.
Out come the sages slowly moving on,
By Hancock led and thoughtful Jefferson.
Him bore Virginia wisest of her men,
Him Freedom chose her potent word to pen.
Of all the Deities that rule above
Her he adored with patriot's warmest love.
Now spread her wings, so widely ne'er before,
Himself should herald her triumphant soar.
With beating heart he stood before the throng,
And thus proclaimed the word desired so long:

"When urged by Fate the righteous cause de-
    mands
The patriot's sword to sever hostile bands,
Hurl from his throne the tyrant, and uprear
The rule of Freedom swayed with love, not fear;
Due deference to influenced mankind
Him asks to open his determined mind.

"These truths we hold:—All men are equal born,
Endowed with rights that never can be lorn;
Among which rights we as the dearest claim
Life, liberty, and happiness's aim.
These to secure were governments ordained,
While with the people all the power remained.
Their creatures those, from whose declared consent
The rule supreme for justice pledged was lent.
Whenever justice dwindles under might
By sovereigns swayed against impartial right,
The subjects can th' obnoxious power efface;
And with a milder government replace.
Prudence, indeed, the people's hand will guide,
And bid not rashly ties long used divide;
Whence teems the page, that earth's events records,
With man's endurance of despotic lords.
But when he groans in hopeless slavery,
To break his fetters Powers supreme decree.

Thus have we borne with England's ruthless king,
Thus are we forced his yoke from us to fling,
And to the world our just complaints we bring.
　"He has rescinded our ancestral laws,
Opposed to plead in civil courts our cause,
Revoked the judgments of our public voice,
And forced to own his foreign wilful choice.
He has reduced our courts to ruffians armed,
Our peaceful trade with murderous hosts alarmed;
Our citizens seized by his pirate band
Compelled to war against their native land;
Our seas has plundered, ravaged all our coasts,
With fire and sword swept o'er our fields his hosts.
He now is gathering to our Briton foe
His Hessian panders to complete our woe;
While on our homes he pours the Indian's rage,
In slaughter nursed, nor sparing sex nor age.
　"Amid these horrors vainly have we cried
For just redress; no pitying voice replied.
Nor Britain's sons have kindred love disclosed,
Leagued with the tyrant, to their kin opposed.
Urged thus by Fate our galling chains we rend,
And swear for life and death our Freedom to de-
　　　fend.
　"We, therefore, trusted with our country's care,
Before all nations solemnly declare,

That no submission to a foreign throne
By Albion held or any king we own;
But that these realms, which common ties unite,
Are Free and Independent States by right;
Th' American Republic be their name,
Our lives we pledge to spread her deathless fame!"
   Sped was the potent word; its magic notes
The breeze receives and o'er the New World floats;
The people hears and one-voiced gladly cries,
Bells high, guns low with rapture rend the skies.
"Fourth of July!" from every lip resounds;
"Fourth of July!" each new-born year rebounds.
The godlike seer beholds the endless line
Of ages worshipping at Freedom's shrine;
Sees Rome and Greece their liberties unveil,
And wild with joy their perfect Offspring hail.
Oppression's shackles drop from every slave,
Rights equal bless and join the good and brave.
No longer patriots persecuted roam,
America is every freeman's home.

CANTO III.

LAND favored by the Gods, who for thee chose
Earth's greatest warrior, when thy cry arose
For Independence, and with arms untrained
Thy cause against skilled hosts should be maintained.
Words are not deeds; each vulgar tongue can bark,
But not each hand can lasting triumphs mark.
From millions rose the clamor to be free,
One arm divine led on to victory.
Him, Alleghania, sing! immortal voice
Alone can praise th' ethereal Powers' choice.
  Thy love, Virginia, mother of the brave,
Our godlike Washington to Freedom gave.
Thy broad Potomac hailed his prosperous birth,
Thy Stafford groves retold his boyish mirth.
From thy fond home he bounded at the peal
Of hostile arms to tempt his youthful steel
In western wilds on Gallia's matchless swords,
And whet his mind on craft of Indian hordes.
Hesperian, Anglo-Saxon, Mohawk, Gaul,
His valor witnessed, and applauded all.

Decked with his country's laurels, and decreed
Against the tyrant all her sons to lead,
Then dawned thy glory, Liberty, and round
Thy chosen hero all thy wishes wound.
Slow be the march, and often the retreat,
When Fabius guides, rings Hannibal's defeat.

Land of the Pilgrims, how thy warriors cheered
The chief, when first he 'mid their ranks appeared!
Bold Mifflin stood around, and skilful Lee,
And cultured Reed, and Gates obligingly.
These gleam like stars around the golden sun;
The eyes of all rest on my Washington.
In godlike beauty, muscular and tall,
Like Saul of old he towered o'er them all.
His limbs were sinewy, broad his swelling chest,
His figure stately, but with ease redressed;
High was his brow, his face supremely fair,
Blue were his eyes, and brown his comely hair.
A sombre sadness o'er his features spread
(Sign of the great, in thoughtful wisdom bred).
His tempered soul, as pure as falling snow,
With reason checked the passions' fiery glow.
When to the troops he spoke, a sweetness mild
Suffused his eyes, and lovingly he smiled;
As if to ope the kindness of his heart,
And to their wishes confidence t' impart.

Plain was his speech, yet eloquent, and fraught
With pleasant phrases and with vigorous thought.
Deficience never could his words revoke,
His deeds transcended always what he spoke.
To call him brave seemed prattling with the air,
Whose soul delighted danger's shock to dare;
Such praise resounds not from the soldier's lips,
When pressed on land to board the welcome ships
The order rings, and last of all his band
The tender-hearted general spurns the land:
"Oh more than father!" thousand voices peal;
Words cease; their rolling tears tell what they feel.
    Such tender scene thy, Brooklyn, isle recalls,
When by our chief expelled from Boston's walls
Th' augmented legions thronged thy fated shore,
And stained it ghastly with our warriors' gore.
"My God!" he cried in fatherly dismay;
"How many brave men must I lose this day!"
Yet fearless wisdom swayed his stricken heart,
And thousands lived by his unconquered art:
From deadly fields athwart the misty deep
He led them safely to the mountain's steep;
Whence, hung in terror o'er Manhattan's brow,
They steeped in blood the revelries of Howe;
Dyed with his Briton and his Hessian vile
Each mantled cliff, each ambush-filled defile

But how shall I recount each wild defeat,
Each Arab stratagem, each wise retreat?
How Jersey's valleys with the outrage rang
Of Rall's dragoons and Donop's lawless gang?
How faithless Lee betrayed his country's cause?
How bastard Howe proposed insidious laws?
All schemes Hesperia's champion repressed;
His own lay hid and prospered in his breast.
How forth they sprang and roused the slumbering State,
The Muse impatient hurries to relate.

December wrapped in gelid night the heaven
O'ercast with clouds by piercing tempests driven.
Clogged with huge icefloats and by torrents swelled
Th' impetuous Delaware his waves impelled
Betwixt his rugged sides, now foaming high
Against th' unwieldy mass, then rushing by
In momentary glee, again inclosed,
Then freed again, resistless though opposed.
Along his western bank, with ice and snow
Decked mournfully, stood ranged in lengthy row
America's vowed champions. Far was traced
Their evening march on knee-deep snows defaced
With blood that trickled from their frozen feet.
Rent were their garments, and the tempest beat
Their breasts exposed, and every breath congealed,
And scarce their stiffened hands their arms could
    wield.

Yet in their breasts true patriotism glows,
And never northwind such an ardor froze.
This cold and secret night their arms demands
To crush at once Oppression's boastful bands,
From Brooklyn's isle t' efface the ghastly stain,
And give to Freedom Jersey's vales again.
High o'er them all their Washington appears;
His look consoles, his word them onward cheers.
"The time is come, my soldiers!" loud he cried;
"Who'll lead us on across the icy tide?"
Forth sprang the mariners of Marblehead,
Men in Atlantic's wintry tempests bred.
They rush into the boats, they guide the braves,
They fight the icefloats, and they stem the waves.
That night the Furies of the deep conspire
With northern Harpies in destructive ire;
The maddened waves their icy volumes rush
Upon the boats their common foe to crush;
In vain! the skilful arm evades the blow,
Or drives them groaning and dispersed below.
Thus when fierce Mars incites his warrior's rage,
Divine Minerva arms her heavenly sage,
They meet; that thunders headlong, this espies
His guardless flank, and all his strength outvies.
Nor kindly Gods their potent aid withheld,
But joined the brave, and Delaware repelled;

Till, safely o'er, their godlike chief around
Full twenty hundred leaped upon the ground.

Three told the morning chime when all were o'er;
The next hour saw them move along the shore
Up steepy hills, through narrowing defiles
And forests vast for thrice three weary miles.
Cold shrilled the storm, fast fell the rattling sleet,
The icy ground slipped 'neath their bleeding feet.
Up spurred a herald sent from Sull'van's band :
"Our arms are drenched; what is our chief's com-
    mand ?"
"Then seize your bayonets, nor turn aside
Ere fall the town!" the chief of men replied.
And instantly the fixèd weapons gleam
On hundred guns their thunders to redeem.

Meanwhile in silent slumber Trenton lay,
Unconscious of th' impending deadly fray.
Her Hessian tyrants from the late carouse
Had dropped their arms and reeling sunk to drowse.
The drunken sentry nodded at his post,
The yager dissolute napped with his host.
In downy bed, and fired with generous wine,
The lecherous Rall slept with his concubine :
A worthy hero of the Hessian school,
He deemed the virtuous brave a pious fool;

4

Each day a fairer strumpet he espied,
And took her home unto his lusty side.
Ne'er felt he happier than in those proud days
He lorded Trenton in his easy ways.
Ten told the morn, before his fumy head
Knew light from dark, and bade him leave his bed.
"Whore, out with you!" he thundered; then displayed
His martial grandeur, and his troops surveyed.
Struck was the drum till every hide was rent,
The hautboys played till all the wind was spent.
He tickled said: "'Tis all we have to do;
Play on! we need not fear the rebel crew!"
Such was our hireling foe; in lustful Rall
See every Hessian, and from one know all.

Now glowed the sky with morning's rosy dawn,
And dazzling gleamed the snows on wood and lawn,
When from the thickets skirting Pennington
Out with his braves rushed heavenly Washington;
Upon the heedless post they fiercely flew,
And men and arms to low destruction threw.
As when on Paraguay's grass-covered plain
A flock of sheep lie round their sleeping swain,
The wary jaguar from his lair descries
The careless shepherd and the tempting prize,
Crouched low he noiselessly and slowly creeps
Till near—high bounding in the air he leaps

Upon the startled fold, and sheep and swain
In mangled carnage stretches o'er the plain:
So sprang our warriors on the Hessian crew,
And guard and captain scarce awakened slew.
Stark heard the shout, and from his bushy lair
Rushed on the rampires washed by Delaware;
The towers sink, the batteries give way,
The foe beholds, and flies in dread dismay.
As when the timid deer by generous hounds
Roused from his sleep o'er hill and valley bounds,
Th' unweary chasers vie his headlong strides,
Hang to his heels, and tear his panting sides:
So roused and pressed the stricken Hessians fly,
So heave their breasts, till cowardly they lie
With backs turned to the foe, and thus ignobly die.
Part reached the town and spread the dire alarm;
Rall, startled, hurried from his chamber warm,
Fell in the saddle, spurred his frightened steed
He knew not whither, nor what men to lead.
" On, grenadiers ! on, forward, march !" he cried;
A few still faithful gathered to his side.
But like a cloud that sweeps resistless on,
Now rushed the hardy van of Washington
Upon the shivering herd; through lane and street
The tumult thickens, and the murdering sleet
Incessant rattles, while a flaming ball
With thunder quickened strikes the boisterous Rall;

Full through his groin the whistling weapon flies,
His blood with entrails mixed his war-horse dyes;
Th' indignant soul darts gushing through the wound,
His livid body tumbles to the ground.
Bereft of leader, smitten with wild fears,
On every side disperse his grenadiers:
On every side the town-encircling foes
With gun and bayonet their flight oppose.
So when the leader of the fleecy train
By lions seized drops on th' infested plain,
The stricken herd in wild confusion leap
This way and that; in vain! each flying sheep
From one escaped another lion draws
From out his lair, and crumbles 'neath his paws.
One thousand Hessians thus to ruin fly,
Yet crouch for mercy, loath as braves to die;
Ignoble chains their trembling hands inclose,
Like slaves they sink beneath their conquering foes.

High from his steed with ghastly wounds o'erlaid,
The godlike Washington the field surveyed.
For twoscore hours no slumber had suffused
His wakeful eyes, and harrowing cares refused.
Now dawned his triumph; his unequalled stroke
Had on th' enslavers turned th' enslaving yoke.
Free was his country; free as ne'er before;
Oppression now could dictate terms no more.

With pious gratitude o'erflows his soul,
The thankful tears in quick succession roll,
His folded hands he raises to the skies:
"My God, thy power has saved our arms!" he cries.
The Power above receives his grateful prayer,
And succoring Fates rush from th' empyreal air.
　　Lo! how on Trenton proud Cornwallis cheers
Erskine's dragoons and Donop's grenadiers!
Too vast their force and fresh from long repose,
With wayworn troops their vanguard to oppose;
Yet flight precipitous must quickly mar
His country's joy from late successful war.
Thinks Washington, when suddenly a light
Of hope illumes him in his sleepless night:
"Up, warriors, follow me!" he says, and guides
Their feet along Assanpink's gloomy sides,
Till, when Aurora gilds the frosty lawn,
Within a league from hostile Princeton drawn
In battle-form they wait Cornwallis' rear,
Which led by Mawhood from the town draws near.
They clash against; fast fly the clicking balls;
Our daring chivalry promiscuous falls:
Neal o'er his cannon, Mercer from his steed,
Fleming and Haslet while they foremost lead
Virginia's sons and those of Delaware.
But not in vain so gallantly they dare.

Bold Hitchcock forward speeds his valiant band,
On rush the riflemen of dauntless Hand;
Before them all the chief of chiefs appears,
His noble form more than his word them cheers;
With him upon the roaring brass they bound,
The gunners seize and dash them to the ground.
Confused at courage more than human fled
Britannia's host to distant Maidenhead;
While our Hesperians triumphing looked down
O'er Jersey's vales from rocky Morristown.

CANTO IV.

ONTARIO's valleys, what terrific gloom
Hung o'er your hamlets and presaged your doom,
When at the foot of Adirondack's mount
Laved by the waters of Bouquet's clear fount
The motley council met!   Near by the waves
Of Champlain chafe and gnaw the rocky caves.
His breast is veiled with wildly fluttering sails
Vast horrors wafting down fair George's vales,
Where high Ticonderoga rears his wall
Ere long to share his northern brother's fall.
Huge pines and hemlocks shades impervious form,
Unbent by age, uninjured by the storm ;
Beloved haunt of Nature's fiercest son,
He courts its silence and its shadows dun,
There meditates the foul and bloody deed,
Thence springs destructive on the blooming mead ;
Where'er he passes ruin's flames arise,
The shrieks of women and the children's cries.
Such fiend, Oppression, should thy arms entwine,
With such red aid should prosper thy design.

My Alleghania, used to Indian art
Of speech and warfare, thy support impart!
'Twas in the moon when berries bend the thorns
And sprouting maize the furrowed fields adorns,
When laky fish in tiny streamlets spawn
And infant rabbits skim across the lawn;
Four hundred braves of Iroquois' fierce race,
And great Algonquin, matchless in the chase,
And lake-bred Ottawa sat on the ground,
With seven thousand Britons ranged around.
Grand was the scene; thy, Champlain, wooded shore
Had never borne such mighty chiefs before;
Alliance such had never tolled the doom
Of brave Hesperia, and prepared her tomb.
Awhile they silent gazed; when Mohawk's chief,
Fierce Brant, thus spoke in accents stern and brief:

"White brothers! we have left our plains to give
Our hands in friendship, and with you to live.
Your foe is ours; the Mohawk's eye can pierce
Through every thicket, and his soul is fierce;
Ten scalps we bring; our knives are keen and red;
We wipe them not till every foe lies dead."

To whom the leader of the British host,
Ostentous Burgoyne, in preposterous boast:

"Thayendanegea, and ye warriors all,
Thronged hither at our common father's call!

With joy hath beat his royal heart to hear
Your loyal love swayed nor by gold nor fear,
E'er since rebellious whites refused to bring
Obedient tribute to our righteous king.
Just vengeance forthwith every breast inspired,
The crying insult all your valor fired;
Yet till your aid the sovereign word ordained,
In meek endurance were your arms restrained.
Divine affection! but no longer now
To ruthless terror can your bravery bow.
Me sends the mighty king to burst the bands
Yourselves imposed with too submissive hands.
Brave warriors, ye are free! your arms unite
With Britain's host and join the glorious fight!
Our brothers ye! thence be our only strife
For battle's laurels and a friendly life.
Joined to our ranks with all your fierceness rush
Upon the rebels and their homesteads crush.
Our duty be to check your boiling ire,
Direct your valor and subdue your fire.
When not opposed by warlike foes, restrain
Your vengeful arms and from all blood refrain;
But smiles or truce or horrid battles rage,
Spare harmless childhood and defenceless age,
And feeble women, and the foe who waives
Th' unequal combat and for mercy craves.

For every captive shall ye gain your prize;
But gory scalps the white man's heart decries.
To Indian braves no fairer spoils appear,
I know your customs and your thoughts revere,
Grant what I can: yours be the gory dead
Struck by your arms; scalp every lifeless head
The wounded only and the dying foe
Be spared the knife and every savage blow.
Base murder, ravage, and destructive flames,
And sexual horror Albion's host disclaims.
Mine be the care to rule the battle-car,
And gently glide, or urge promiscuous war.
Rest ye contented; should rebellion's hands
Outrage a brave of our allianced bands,
Your inborn vengeance I no more restrain;
Retort the deed and crowd their homes with slain!"
  He said, and solemnly his seat retook;
Whom Iroquois' first chieftain thus bespoke:
  "We greet thee as our father; for in thee
Our mighty father's voice across the sea
We hear. The whites of Boston long have tried
To gain the Indian warriors to their side;
But we have loved thy father, and our darts
Have barbed and sharpened on our loving hearts.
In sign of which our chiefs and warriors all
Have left their villages t' obey thy call.

None but the wounded and in wars grown old
And squaws and little ones our wigwams hold.
One heart is ours; we offer thee our hands
To keep thy words and do thy just commands.
So the Great Spirit may thy power raise,
And slay thy foes, and give thee length of days!"
   Barbarian yells the muffled stillness tear,
And lowering woes to peaceful homesteads bear.
To stamp the fate, the fraughtful calumet
With eagle-claws and human headskins set,
From lip to lip successive passed around,
And breathing slaughter smoked along the ground.
Then spread the feast: Britannia's savage store
Each bosom tortures with the lust of gore,
As writhe the entrails with the watery fire,
And rouse the man-beast to the fierce desire.
Oh, ancient God! thy frenzies were a calm;
To modern Bacchus yield the drunkard's palm!
That Indian youth who mixed with Europe's maid,
And fire and slaughter for her lust repaid.
Say, Burgoyne, whither fly thy vaunting words?
Are Mohawk tomahawks like English swords?
When on our homes thy human beasts of prey
Were let devouring, did they merely slay
Thy pointed victims, or did maid and wife
In mingled carnage sink beneath their knife?

Immortal Gods! how rings the piercing wail!
Haste, Alleghania, knoll the direful tale!
On Hudson's banks, where Stoney's purling rill,
From rock to rock skims down the pine-crowned hill,
Atween the trees an humble cottage gleams
With oaken roofing and with beechen beams;
Two little windows welcome in the day,
One lockless door the wanderer bids to stay.
Ah! many a such recalled the dwellers there,
The warlike brother and the sister fair;
How he would ask him rest his weary feet,
And she would bring him beverage cool and sweet.
May be he tarried, not so much to rest,
As to obey the longings of his breast:
For who could see that face divinely fair,
Those deep-black eyes, those locks of jetty hair,
And watch those lips when words harmonious flowed,
And how those cheeks with maiden blushes glowed;
But owned his soul drawn to the form divine,
And pleasing heard a voice: "Ah! were she mine!"
Yet Crema, while with modest grace she served
Each welcome guest, one hallowed flame preserved.
Thine, David, was her love; whom childlike play
Had long united in affection's sway.
Already youthhood eyed the nuptial heaven,
When, ah! by war each tender tie was riven:

Mistaken zeal to Britain's legions drew
The warlike youth; to Canada he flew,
Thence shining in the ranks of hostile war,
But mourning o'er his stricken spouse afar.
Two years thus passed; when Burgoyne's motley band
In ruin swept Ontario's fertile land:
Wild rumor flew before his savage van,
From field and hamlet fled defenceless man.
Fair Crema's fate her brother's succor calls,
To shield his charge he seeks Albania's walls;
Thence urges flight from Hudson's threatened vales,
And to secure retreat his sister hails.
Still she refrained, withheld by stronger tie
To where Fort Edward reared his turrets high:
There in the British camp her lover whiled,
There union checked so long enchanting smiled;
No ruthless hand her innocence could harm,
Whose safety rested on such soldier's arm.
    Ah, fated maid! how vain are all thy dreams!
How sadly artless all thy fondest schemes!
From savage breasts to every pity steeled
What brave or sage could tempting captive shield?
While still deluded thus with fond desires,
Too late she eyes Destruction's horrid fires
On every side lay waste great Hudson's lands,
And sex and age fall 'neath remorseless hands.

Impending woes now urge her instant flight
Amid the stillness of the moonless night.
Already stand her feet prepared, when lo!
Bursts the frail door, and in the torch's glow
Blood-painted Indian faces fiercely glare
With wanton glee upon their victim fair.
She wildly shrieks; in vain! the chieftain's knife
Whirls o'er her head, impatient for her life.
Yet stays a moment; gleams a hopeful ray
In Crema's breast, and opes her lips to pray:
"Oh brave! awhile thy furious arm restrain,
Nor madly spurn the prize of plenteous gain!
A youthful chief shares thy own camp above,
David his name, and I his chosen love.
Lead me to him: his spouse if he behold
Safe at thy hands, what gifts will he unfold!
Tobacco, weapons, and refulgent gold!"
Pleased Giengwahtoh sunk his wampum blade,
And for the ransom spared the praying maid.
Thus the fierce Turk, inspired with faithful zeal,
O'er some fair captive wields his crooked steel,
When eft recurs his meretricious lord,
Whose glittering gold restrains the vengeful sword.
The war-chief's words his warriors' fury damp;
Keen for the prize they hasten to the camp.
  Fair Crema's tender longings warmer grew
As to her lover's home she nearer drew;

Little she recked the savage-looking band,
Her wearied foot, the cord that griped her hand;
Already gleamed on Edward's distant plain
The tents of Albion and her brazen train.
"Soon shalt thou see thy lover!" said the chief;
"But rest awhile, and give thy feet relief!"
A bubbling fountain issued from the ground;
There with the maid the warriors sat around.
Flagitious rest! which rouses fierce desire
Not slaked with water, but incensed with fire.
Their savage throats the flaming torrent swill,
Wild roll their eyes, blood-lusts their bosoms fill.
Each gazes round and sees a brother fiend,
Each eyes the maiden innocent, unscreened:
"Whose squaw is this?" forgetful they demand.
"Not squaw, but maid espoused to David's hand;
Her prize is fixed;" chief Giengwahtoh cries.
"And who," they ask, "will gain the promised prize?"
At which the chief enraged: "Who whirled the knife,
The maiden's prayer heard, and spared her life?
Mine is the prize!" Yells of defiance rise;
Their armed hands quiver; fiercely roll their eyes.
Fell Giengwahtoh reads their wild desires,
A hellish thought his savage breast inspires:
"Braves!" yells he; "thus we end the raging strife:
Nor mine the prize, nor yours, but mine her life!"

And rushing on the shrieking maid he grasped
Her beauteous locks, and while she faintly gasped
"Oh David!" plunged with soothless fury pressed
The stony knife into her panting breast.
White turn her jetty eyes, and from the wound
Her heart's pure gore spouts on the green-turfed ground.
Gods! yet no pity? did ye e'er impart
Such human sense to Indian's brutal heart?
Still flows the blood, and from the brow divine
He tears the scalp, and rears the gory sign.
As the fell tiger from his bushy mound
Leaps on the roe and strikes her to the ground,
With cutting paw divides the bleeding mesh,
Quaffs the warm blood, and grinds the quivering flesh,
Cloyed, o'er his back the mangled rest he flings,
And as a trophy to his family brings:
Thus to his wampum-belt the war-chief tied
Fair Crema's scalp blood-dyeing all his side,
Then yelling fiercely to the camp he flew,
And under Britain's eyes the ghastly booty threw.
   Ah! who can tell what fearful pangs arise
In David's breast, as thus his spouse he eyes!
How shake his hands as with unknown despair
They stroke that crimsoned skin, that clotted hair!
Oh, Muse, thy theme forsake! let love-led hands
Rest Crema's corse in Hudson's mourning sands!

Her silken hair sleep on her lover's breast,
Till weeping floods his eyelids drown to rest !
All-ruling Gods the horrid death allowed
To stamp with shame eterne the cruel proud.
In vain Britannia washed her bloody hands,
In vain soft Burgoyne checked his savage bands ;
The stain adhered like leopard-spots impressed,
The murderer lived at Luc's and Albion's guest.
But vainly not America surveyed
Her kindling hosts, and vengeful ranks arrayed ;
The maiden's blood, by British arts decreed,
Of fiery valor sprouts the fruitful seed.

5*

CANTO V.

WHEN from Ontario's lake his deer-skin sails
The Indian spreads for Mohawk's verdant vales,
Into Oswego's billowy stream he guides
His bark-canoe up where the pine-crowned sides
Of that bright river part awhile to grace
The sleeping beauty of Oneida's face,
Thence through the Forest Brook, till gently nigh
The adverse pines entwine their branches high:
Here shallows thwart the liquid way awhile,
Auspicious waters parts a woodland mile;
The son of Nature lifts his light canoe,
The sun scarce varied sees him row anew
On Mohawk's waters laughing 'tween the vales
He sought so strangely with his deer-skin sails.
Thus long ago, ere foreign feet had trod
With noisy step the redman's sacred sod,
Was done the wondrous voyage; but when pealed
The battle great through Mohawk's hunting-field,
Devoted sons of Liberty descried
The lordly spot that checked the favorite tide,

Upon whose waves insidious Britain poured
On southern plains her northern savage horde.
A rampire vast the site already walled,
Schuyler its name, by ancients Stanwix called,
Just where from lurking woods the stealthy brave
Launched his canoe on Mohawk's murmuring wave.
Ontario's sons the sturdy bastions manned
With levelled thunders and their fearless band ;
Stout-hearted Gansevoort their ardor swayed,
Eight hundred braves his gentle word obeyed.

Sight loved by Gods ! when chief and warriors bend
Their arms united to the selfsame end ;
In vain two thousand motley weapons flew
Against the walls from Albion's hybrid crew:
British and Hessian, loyalist white and red,
By green-clad Johnson and grim Leger led.
The weary siege their warlike fire depressed,
Desponding fears their drooping souls possessed.
Already dawned the leaguered band's relief,
As stealthily approached Ontario's chief,
The dauntless Herkimer, with Tryon's men
Slow winding through Oriska's bushy glen.
And had not Fates averse their aid withheld,
Oppression's host his storm had not repelled.
But patriot gore must fertilize the ground
Ere sprouts the tree with Freedom's blossoms crowned.

Such is the will of Gods; and thus awhile
They seem to favor tyrants with their smile;
Rest we content; 'tis naught but the design
Of heavenly powers to form their wrath divine.
Thus Neptune, when against some lawless crew
Incensed he bids the deeps their horrors brew,
First o'er the seas a gentle calm prepares
To lull their cares and strike them unawares,
Sudden the whirling hurricane he pours
Athwart the deep; sea, air, and heaven roars;
The smitten crew scarce own the vengeful arm,
So quick the change, so sudden the alarm;
But pressed like sheep that prowling wolves appall,
They rush together, o'er each other fall,
Linked deadly fast, till ruin gulps them all.

When was a plan devised, and not a spy
Pricked up his ear and keened his lurking eye?
Through the dark swale as on the leaf-strewn ground
With cautious step the succoring patriots wound,
A squaw's far-piercing eye lay on them bent,
Hung on their lips and read their whole intent;
Fierce Branta she, the Mohawk's sister dire,
Nursed in his schemes and flaming with his ire.
Sent to the woods to watch the suspect foe,
She from a hill had spied his ranks below.

Quick as her mind the deep design revealed,
She sped her word to Schuyler's battle-field.
At once the din of barbarous war resounds,
The lusty Indian to the combat bounds,
Each more than other anxious for the fray,
In bloody quaffs his thirsty soul t' allay;
Scarce half the host before the walls remain,
Nor threats nor force their fury can restrain.

Say, Muse, what chieftains led the savage band?
What heroes flocked to Herkimer's command?
By Watts were Johnson's green-clad Yorkers led,
The ranging troops by him who basely fled
From Freedom's cause, vile Butler; next appeared
Canadian forest-men by Claudian cheered;
Bird soldier-like his well-trained squadrons drew;
Brant fiercely yelling with his warriors flew
In wild confusion, nor with other aim
Than first of all to reap barbarian fame.
Still winding through Oriska's dark defile
Tryonia's braves in close-compacted file
Their dauntless leader followed; gaily shone
The arms of Paris and his war-like son,
Impatient in the van; Cox urged the hour;
Bold Spencer stalked in conscious manly power.
Ah, noble blood! by Fate's all-ruling hand
Decreed t' enlive the glories of your land!

Oh, may you not have been effused in vain!
May never age efface your glorious stain!
Your seed forever sprout on Freedom's plain!
   'Twas at the hour when tender wives prepare
For husbands labor-worn the noonday fare;
By murky clouds lay hid the summer sun,
As if the impending rage of blood to shun:
Sudden through all Oriska's forest rung
The savage yell; off ball and arrow sung;
From either hill, in front, on every side
Rushed on the glen Britannia's murderous tide.
As when his fleecy charge the western swain
Leads through a wood to reach a grassy plain,
In case secure, straightway as from the sky
The spotted panther from his tree on high
Darts on the stricken fold at unawares,
And fiercely throws and strikes and cuts and tears:
So unforeseen and fierce on Tryon's men
Of danger thoughtless marching through the glen
Bursts the wild rush of horror from the hills,
And all their van with dread and slaughter fills.
What hero first stretched on th' ensanguined plain?
Impetuous Cox; warmed in his quivering brain
The feathered weapon stuck; eternal shade
Enshrouds his eyes; he bites the leafy glade.
Young Paris next was doomed to share his fall;
Shivering his ribs, the ranger's whistling ball

Fast sought his heart, there lodged; prone on the
    ground
The warrior sinks; his glittering arms resound.
  As the bold lion, suddenly when pressed
By dogs and hunters, feels his lordly breast
Flutter awhile with fear; aroused he burns
With honest shame, all danger proudly spurns,
The yelping curs to this and that side flings,
With jaws distended on the huntsman springs:
So Tryon's braves, first reeling 'neath the shock,
Quick roused their souls, and like a mountain rock
Immovable their bristling van they form,
And calmly stand the furies of the storm.
Death, e'er impartial, turned his wonted course,
On Britain's legions bursts his murdering force.
By Spencer's dart was traitorous Watson slain,
His throat-pierced carcass tumbled to the plain.
Vile Butler's son 'neath Younglove's hatchet fell,
His vulgar soul howled to the shades of hell.
Through Ingelow's groin Gardinier's arrow sped,
The ghastly wound his smoking entrails shed;
Eternal night the youthful soul invades,
That flies disdainful to the Stygian shades.
  High on his war-horse, like a tower upreared,
The pride of Tryon, Herkimer, appeared;
Him Mohawk's valley to his country gave,
From Alemannia came his fathers brave.

Like ancestry his followers impart,
Teutons in look, Americans in heart;
Not that degenerate race by tyrants hired,
But men reborn, with Liberty inspired.
Heavens! what heaps of slain uptowers that arm!
How shrinks the foe and cowers with alarm!
Proud Watts indignantly the brave descries,
With rage he foams, wrath sparkles in his eyes,
Full at his breast the levelled tube he brings,
Bursts the quick flame, the wingèd lead-stone sings—
Then had thy glory, Tryon, sunk to rest;
But kind Minerva shields the hero's breast—
The thwarted ball fell furious on his horse,
Cut his fair neck and stretched his giant corse,
Below the knee the chief's leg shivering rent,
Then far in empty air its fury spent.
With grateful tears the veteran brave confessed
The arm divine and smote his thankful breast.
"Warriors!" he cried; "not yet I leave the field,
While Powers above the sons of Freedom shield;
Beneath yon beech your wounded general lay,
There will I rest, and watch the bloody fray!"
　　His trusty warriors do the work of love;
The tender sight melts all the Powers above.
Jove bent the sanguine Briton to dismay
And add new glories to the doubtful day,

Shook the wide heavens with his awful nod
Whence burst the fire and thunder of the God.
Full on the foe the howling tempest blew,
The sulphurous streaks into their faces flew.
Vainglorious Watts stands blinded by the flame,
He gropes about a sad and deadly aim.
Him Spencer eyed, and at his reeling head
Levelled the bow; the whizzing arrow sped
Between the eye and nose, the nerves unstrung,
Rushed through the head, and grimly quivering hung;
The bleeding eyeball issues from the wound;
Supine the warrior tumbles to the ground.
Brave Bird beheld, and kindling at the sight
His marshalled Albions thundered to the fight,
Spencer his aim; full at the hero's heart
Twice fifteen guns their fiery shower dart;
Forward he falls, his face turned to the foe,
His right still grasps the dart, his left the bow.
Thus the grim lion, undisturbed by fears,
Though pierced all through with closely trembling
     spears,
No step retreats, but opes his lordly breast
To newer wounds, till in his heart impressed
His dauntless soul they free, and sink his corse to rest.
   Around the dead the madding tumult grows,
In wild confusion mingle friends and foes;

Roused to revenge by heaps of stricken braves
On either white the tawny savage raves.
As the fierce tiger driven from his den
By yelping dogs and troops of armèd men,
Though herds of sanguine leopards quickly grow
Around his side to fight the common foe,
Spurns every aid that alien succor lends,
And all but tiger to his fury bends :
So the wild Indian, when with rage he burns,
None but his own amid the host discerns ;
Or Briton or Hesperian be the white,
An equal wrath inflames the hated sight.
Thus on themselves Britannia's leaguers call
Th' inhuman rage roused for another's fall.
While bitter factions more than tyrant's love
Her recreant minions to the combat move :
Each loyal wretch his former neighbor's fame
In yonder patriot sees and his own shame.
There on the ground in death's fierce struggle clasped
The lifeless combatants still firmly grasped
Each other's hair, and at each other's breast
The reeking weapon undissevered pressed.
So when the lion and the tiger meet,
Too noble that, too fierce this to retreat,
Their power the same, awhile they sternly stare
In challenge mute, then cleave the separate air

With levelled paw; their striped and yellow hides
Give the black gore; bare lie their panting sides;
They cuff, they roar, they tear, they cut, they strike
With equal force, with rage impelled alike;
Till fastening on the neck's arterial vein
Dying and dead locked fast they thunder to the plain.
    Insatiate thus the bloody combat burns
While noon to eve the flying orb returns.
Already Britain's rangers drop their guns,
Avoidless death the fiercest Indian shuns;
Sudden from Schuyler's walls quick thunders sound,
From every side foes seem to rush around:
On green and red-clad troops a deadly fright
Falls with the clap; they rush to vulgar flight.
Mohawk and Seneca despairing cry:
"Oonah! Oonah!" and to the forest fly;
E'en Brant and Red-Coat shudder at the fray,
Beat their rough breasts, and yelling dash away.
America's unconquered braves surround
Their dying leader glorious on the ground.
"General!" they cry; "our country's field is won!"
"Thank God!" he sighs; "no more desires her son.
Hand me the flag!" He pressed it to his breast,
Kissed the loved sign, and calmly sunk to rest.
Where is his grave? In every patriot's heart.
What monumental words his deeds impart?

"Brave Herkimer, Oriska's hero, first
The gloomy scene of northern wars reversed,
Who not for gain, but for his country's love,
Oppression fought; his only prize above!"
Immortal Washington thus spake his praise,
Whose words transcend e'en Alleghania's lays.

CANTO VI.

GREEN Mountains! how your sight my boyhood
    cheered,
When clad in Fancy's tinctured robe appeared
Your rounded summits lifting to the skies
Those lordly trees whose garb no winter dies!
Enraptured gazed I on your winding creeks
Bounding from rock to rock in playsome freaks
Adown your sloping sides, then moving slow
In silver clearness through the vales below.
But fairer far appeared your virgin scene,
With brighter rapture glowed my bardic mien,
When all along your verdant woodlands rung
Our Freedom's war-drum, and like pines upsprung
From every peak your ardent Boys to trace
In mountain chivalry their warlike race
From Caledonia's highland chiefs of yore,
Whose shrill horn silenced all Britannia's roar.
Immortal race! whose sons in Stark return
On Bennington the Bruce of Bannockburn!
    Vermont's fair sister, she whom wanderers name
America's Helvetia, with the same

Upsoaring mountains decked, whose honors white
The gazer's eye and reader's mind delight,
Bore Stark to Freedom. Him while still a boy
The hunter's rambles and adventures joy:
Up Merrimac's clear stream his skiff to row
And draw the salmon from his ooze below,
Or roam the shades of Strafford's forests drear
And track the footprints of the flying deer.
Nor savage beasts his boyish ardor stay;
More savage men entice him to the fray.
As pristine Sparta taught her hopeful race
First to essay th' adventures of the chase;
To spread the net, to shape the barbèd dart,
To draw the bow (first parts of sylvan art),
The bounding stag to press along the shore,
Perched on the cliff to face the bristling boar;
Then on marauding bands their valor proved,
And last their arms against the phalanx moved:
So her fair daughter, my unequalled land,
To th' arm of soldier nursed the angler's hand;
From trout to deer, from beast to manly foe,
To gun and cannon from the line and bow
She trained her offspring, while the glorious State
Formed fast divinely by the hand of Fate.
Thus grew my Stark, inured to early strife,
His home the forest, jeopardy his life.

Not yet his sixteenth winter's frosts he bore,
When on Winnipiseogee's northern shore
While for the furry game he spread the snare,
Sudden a weighty hand griped fast his hair;
And looking up twelve braves he eyed around,
Who quickly bound him thrust unto the ground.
Thence to their home, where meet two rivers bright,
Francis the less, the greater Lawrence hight,
Was dragged the beardless youth, and for six weeks
Pained with the savages' inhuman freaks.
Released with price enormous from the band
By Massachusetts' ever friendly hand
He toiled to pay his ransom by the chase
Of Androscoggin's fur-prized beaver-race.
Then pealed the nobler call—ah, nobler far
Than ever summoned heroes to the war!
Severely cultured Stark at once the call
Obeyed, and hastened to the tyrant's fall.
To Medford's field, up Bunker's Hill he sprung;
From ice-clogged Delaware his triumph rung.
Vermont now travails to complete his fame,
Inscribing on her highest cliff his name;
That when the wanderer views her Mountains Green,
A monumental Stark may daze his mien.
What sped contending armies to yon heights
So long reposing in secure delights?

Wild rumor talked to Burgoyne's willing ears
Of numerous war-horses and fattened steers,
Of maize, wheat, barley heaped in massive stores,
Of cannon-chariots ranged in fifty scores—
All congregated in small Bennington,
The wealthiest spot warmed by Hesperian sun.
Quick as the bruit the Briton urged away
His motley minions on th' enticing prey.
In vain he urged, when Baum sedate and slow
Such hybrids led against one ardent foe.
Tenscore dragoons limped on without a steed
(The steeds still grazed on Bennington's fat mead),
Of Hanau fifty tugged two brazen guns,
As many marksmen joined of Albion's sons,
Twice fifty Tories and Canadians drew
With hundred Indians mixed in one wild crew.
Such moved Britannia's glory, whom ere long
With tardy Breymann tracked an equal throng;
So slow their march, that for one weary mile
A tedious hour their Hessian footsteps while.

But zeal impetuous the warriors fires
Whom love of country and of home inspires.
Scarce Cambridge shook with Baum's unformed alarms
Than all Vermont and Hampshire flew to arms.
From every cliff of Mountains Green and White
The rural patriot rushes to the fight.

Thus Cincinnatus leaning on his spade,
Roused at the call his threatened country made,
Shook off the dust, and: "Haste, Racilia!" cried;
"My toga bring!" Th' obsequious partner sighed,
Yet not restrained his higher love; away
The rustic hero thundered to the fray:
So great in war, scarce thence of Æquian race
On Anio's stream remained a single trace.
All hail, ye Roman Goddesses! who bore
Such Cincinnati to our blessed shore!

From olden monuments, my Maid divine,
Record some names of that heroic line!
With hundred men from Berkshire Symonds sped,
A double force the gallant Nichols led,
Hubbard and Stickney joined with power the same,
Three hundred more with valorous Herrick came;
Still on the march brave Warner's Hampshire toils,
Though not too late to reap the glorious spoils;
Stark led the van; whate'er be other names,
All were Americans, all Freedom claims.

Th' auspicious day appeared. No cloudy bars
Closed the blue sky farewelling night's last stars.
Green Mountain's pine-tops first the golden rays
Caught on their branches laughing in the blaze,
As smiles a maiden rosy-cheeked and fair
When darts a splendor from her pearly hair.

Brighter and brighter glowed the mountain's head,
Till through the trees opposed the God-Son spread
His spotless bosom partly veiled, then raised
His flaming eyes, and on the valley gazed
In proud survey; where eager for his light
The bold Hesperians panting sought the fight.
Pleased at their wish Apollo quickly reared
His form on high, and all displayed appeared.
Full thousand tongues his bright assistance hail:
Now to the fight! no more restraints avail!
Stark mounts his war-horse, draws his trusty sword,
His eager warriors fires with Spartan word:
"Now on, my men! The red-coats there you see!
Ere night they fall, or ground their arms, or flee;
Else Molly's love must ever grieve for me!"
  No shouts arise; for all their chief obeyed,
Intent to conquer with the martial Maid.
Sure source of triumph! They who rashly throw
By Mars impelled their vigor on the foe,
Can seldom conquer; only countless graves
Mark either host, when Enyalius raves.
But when Minerva lifts her prudent spear,
The fiercest foe is struck with powerless fear;
By her assisted Diomed e'en won
Th' unequal strife o'er Jove's immortal son;
Full at the God the daring weapon flew,
From his rent groin the blood celestial drew;

Mad with the pain fierce Mavors roared aloud,
And fled in shame behind Olympus' cloud.
Thus fame and glory grace Minerva's sons
From ancient Ithaci to modern Washingtons.
Stark not the least: by her inspired he sent
His soldiers singly round the battlement
By Albion's host raised on the sloping hill
Whose basis laves Walloomscoick's winding rill.
Like farmers clad, when in the sunburnt fields
They cut the crops that bounteous Ceres yields,
With guns in hand, no bayonets attached,
They stole around the hill in bands detached.
Nichols' and Herrick's men thus toward the rear
Approached; two hundred more in front drew near
By Hubbard led and Stickney. Not a sign
Of hostile strategy the foes divine.
Unskilful Skene convinced phlegmatic Baum,
They were but loyal farmers who had come
From far and near his shelter to request.
Thus blinds imprudence whom the Gods detest.
    But Nature's sons, in circumvention nursed,
The happy stratagem eftsoons dispersed.
"The woods are full of Yankees !" ring their yells
In fiendish discord with their jingling bells
(Strange tocsins !) ; from the mound they rush between
The rural patriots now unmaskèd seen.

In vain to safety urge their nimble feet;
A blood-drenched pathway marks their base retreat.
Ignoble Ottawas! no daring hand
Could shame eternal banish from your band?

In favoring splendor on his noonday throne
The gold-haired Godhead now serenely shone;
When toward the foe confused with dire alarm
Stark high in air upraised his valorous arm:
"Forward!" he cried; and all in front and rear,
On right and left, the surging squadrons near.
As up the cliffs that skirt Jamaica's shores
The direful hurricane tumultuous roars,
The huge mahoganies their sturdy age
In vain oppose, they crumble 'neath his rage:
Thus on the Briton's close and frowning stakes
Our highland host with crushing fury breaks.
The rampire falls; swift o'er the smoking space
Vermont the foe encounters face to face.
Nor stakes nor mounds the leaden death arrest;
Free leaps the ball straight at the soldier's breast.
Should Jove his thunder ceaselessly prolong
For two full hours, thus stopless and thus long
The cannon's roar, the musket's clicking shook
The downtrod hill, the blood-discolored brook.
Baum bravely stood; though wavering and slow
In open war he never turned from foe.

His cannon twain upreared on high supplied
Full hundred guns, and all the host defied.
Stark saw indignantly, and calling loud
His highland boys rushed on the fire-charged cloud
Scarce eight yards distant; down the cannoneers
Dropped on their brands, and swift the mountaineers
Manned the fierce thunder. All unarmed the foe
Now fly dispersed and seek the woods below.
Baum only stands; too brave to spurn the field,
Too proud a soldier e'en in death to yield,
He whirls his sword against the victors all,
Bold, though in vain; fast flies the deadly ball
Into his noble heart; prone to the ground
He falls, in shades eternal wrapped around.

Yet Liberty for fairer triumph longed,
While Sol attentive still his light prolonged.
Scarce Baum's defeat all Bennington had cheered,
When lumbering Breymann on the field appeared
With twice two hundred Hessians, quickly swelled
By sorry fugitives with hope impelled.
Stark first beheld; at once the alarum pealed,
And called the victors scattered o'er the field
In quest of booty; quick they rally round
Their stalwart captain thundering from the mound:
" On, boys, for Warner haste ! or we'll lose all !"
Brave Warner just came up to hear his call.

With generous zeal his youthful soldiers glow
To whet, though late, their courage on the foe.
Nor vain their zeal, nor their assistance late;
Without their arms what might have been our fate?
Our victors wearied, scattered o'er the field!
The sturdy Hessians suddenly revealed!
But Warner's mountaineers all fresh, though few,
Like hungry lions on the hybrids flew.
Then rose each highland youth (I give no name;
For all were heroes, all my homage claim!)
In heavenly power (which the Gods bestow),
And with one shock hurled all the foe below.
No valorous thought these timid bosoms swelled,
They only fled and stumbled, bled and yelled.
From field to wood, from vale to hill they ran,
The bravest hero he that led the van.
Yet Breymann felt a spark of soldier pride,
And now and then would turn the coward tide
Back on the foe and to the combat force;
Thus sudden checked great Stark's impetuous horse
Met the swift death, with mute affection eyed
His noble master, gasped once more, and died.
Incensed the chieftain flew on foot along,
Broke each attack, and swelled the dying throng;
Till Phœbus pleased withdrew his final ray,
And peaceful night suppressed the bloody fray.

Then fair Vermont, secure from dreaded foes,
Her valiant sons invited to repose.
Gates plucked the fruit of Stark and Herkimer
In vaunting Burgoyne eft as prisoner
Driven with his northern host's depressed remains
Beneath the yoke on Saratoga's plains.
There stands the trophy; but the spoils were won
At dark Oriska and bright Bennington.

CANTO VII.

Oh, Alleghania! if for bardic lore
Harsh words and low revilement oft I bore,
If for the Muses' and my country's love
I never flinched my zealousness to prove;
Now that thy presence half my toils hath blessed,
Guide me, oh guide me still throughout the rest!
Naught more I dread than in so grand a theme
Aught trivial should obscure thy heavenly gleam.
Raise then my thoughts, and first incite me on
To press the prints of godlike Washington.

In Fabian arts, so little wont to cheer
A headlong senator, had passed the year.
"I cannot bear," cried Adams, "who advise
This shifting war our modern Fabius tries!"
"Thee, Gates!" bawled Lovell, "all the people claim;
Not him who wheels and turns with coward shame!"
Gates pleasing heard: a selfish upstart, all
Intent to rise upon a better's fall.
His country's fate a frivolous affair
Appeared to him, could he but freely share

The highest honors and the fattest spoils;
For this he bore whate'er of warfare's toils.
Intriguers never grumbling creatures need:
Wayne, Mifflin, Conway, Sullivan and Reed
With babbling Wilkinson in low cabal
Joined jealous Gates to urge the hero's fall.
Thus by great chiefs and senators opposed
The undiverted leader still reposed
In calm divine; his trust in God above,
His faith unshaken in his people's love.
From warrior, patriot rose one mighty voice:
" None but our Washington shall be our choice!"
When through the ranks he passed sedate and high,
Love filial sparkled in each soldier's eye.
When rumor spread the general was near,
Crowds filled the roads his sweet approach to cheer.
E'en Britain looked with undissembled frown
On bloody Brandywine and Germantown;
Where, though superior numbers forced retreat,
To them adhered the stigma of defeat.
Truth, Hope and Love inwreathed their fairest bay
Round him who saved his country by delay.

But now bleak winter bade the battle cease,
And seek a shelter in his dreary peace.
The city fair, whose slumbers first awoke
That magic word which slavery's shackles broke,

Now gave, alas! (thus cruel Fates decreed!)
A snug abode to Albion's motley breed.
Here in a dome, there in a sacred fane
The snorting war-horse champed the golden grain;
Soldier and strumpet stained in lustful ball
The reverend floor of Independence Hall;
While Howe, secluded from true valor's fame,
In Andre's pageant glorified his shame.
Away from these, my Muse! and lead me where
Our brave Hesperians winter's horrors bear!
Twice myriad paces from the foe's abode
On Schuylkill's western bank the Chester road
Reveals a valley, then with trees o'erspread
Of massive height and thickness.　Thither led
By ever anxious Washington our few
Surviving warriors raised their homesteads new.
Fast 'neath their axe the towering forest dropped
This way and that; the trunks, shorn bare and lopped
Of branchy crowns, upraised a square-like frame
Formed rudely grand; hewn into slabs the same
Fixed on green rafters made the roof; with clay
Were filled the openings, winter's blasts to stay;
Logs likewise covered o'er with slimy earth
A chimney formed to ope the genial hearth.
Thus hundred cabins in two toilsome days
Our hardy patriots then could ably raise.

Ah! how they needed those now scorned abodes!
For miles around were stained the frozen roads
With blood that trickled from their shoeless feet.
No clothes they had to ward the icy sleet
From off their naked breasts, no tents to keep
Away the storm, no blankets for their sleep.
Now by their toils and tender chieftain's care
Somewhat at least of comfort they could share:
Though stretched on rough-hewn logs, the homely roof
Shut out the snow and kept the storm aloof;
And all exposed their breasts and wounded feet
Could feel the blessings of the log-fire's heat.

 Among those faces, some with many a scar
Made reverend, others scarcely tanned by war,
One with superior features marked I meet,
Pale, thin and worn, sad, resolute, yet sweet
To all surrounding; whatsoever grief
That youthful brow may darken, for relief
It looketh elsewhere, nor with private pain
Will for a moment social mirth restrain.
All knew the youth; Laodon was his name;
Six months had passed since to their ranks he came
From Susquehanna's grove-clad fields to dare
The foe, and Chester's bloody toils to share.
Loved by his general, by all revered
For modest courage, yet to none appeared

The cause whence sadness often gloomed his face;
For none his previous hidden life could trace.
A maiden young and fair, Anella hight,
For years had been his love and sole delight.
Blue were her eyes, her cheeks like roses red,
Her Grecian mouth a blooming fragrance shed;
In light-brown ringlets fell her silken hair
Adown her neck like ivory smooth and fair;
Her hands were white and soft; her little feet
Scarce touched the ground, they were so light and fleet
In gait all noble; slender, full of grace
Her form of artifice shunned every trace.
As God had made her, such she was; untried
Were duly scorned by her those charms applied
T' allure the fop with fineries and slimes
By maids as live in these degenerate times.
Hence eke intent her love to none t' impart
But such whose manly form a noble heart
Bore to return a like, though many came,
None but Laodon won her virgin flame.
Already Hymen's blissful hour drew nigh,
When Howe's near host dissevered every tie.
Their fields and hearths from war's distress to spare
Each man and youth must battle's horrors share.
Laodon warmed the dire appeal t' obey,
Impelled by Freedom to the doubtful fray.

Nor sweet Anella, though intense alarm
Shook all her frame, withheld his generous arm.
Her country's weal required the sacrifice;
She gave her all, though death requite the price.
Thus suddenly their breasts were torn apart,
But not their hearts; they had one only heart,
Which beat alike on Susquehanna's vale,
On Chester's fields and in his dreary swale.
He who can love, no more will marvel now
Anella's grief, Laodon's clouded brow.

    One gloomy morn, with sorrow rent his heart,
He left his comrades, and withdrew apart
To where a rocky-bedded streamlet rills
Atween a glen o'ercapped by wooded hills.
There on a rock he sat him down immersed
In tearful dole, and all his woes rehearsed;
First lowly sighing, then, as if to vent
His burdened soul, thus spake his soft lament:

    "Oh cruel Zephyr, thou, whose happy gales
Waft hourly o'er fair Susquehanna's vales!
Hast thou not told them to inquire for me
Of her whom vainly I desire to see?
Fast on they rush, unmindful of my fears;
They have no heart for lovers' sighs and tears.

    "Here in laments I waste the days so long,
In tearful sighs the sleepless nights prolong;

Oh, my Anella! couldst but thou be here,
How changed would all the gloomy world appear!
Then days and nights would alway be too brief;
I scarce should know the very sense of grief.

  "What pure delights late summer's evening beam
Viewed shed o'er us, as seated by the stream
Low murmuring on we twined our longing arms
In blissful love, rapt in each other's charms!
All shone serene, life's future brewed no cloud;
Now all is dark, hope withers in her shroud.

  "Were I a youth like many youths have been,
Wert thou a maid like many maids are seen,—
Change might allure our eyes to other sights,
Divert our hearts to other soft delights;—
But no! spare my distress! what have I said?
Heaven knows! our hearts are one, alive or dead.

  "In thee, Anella! all my soul's at rest,
My thoughts and wishes never leave thy breast.
Thou know'st how well we alway could agree,
How oft thou saidst: 'God made me all for thee!'
Oh, come, Anella! come! I rush away;
I must see thee, or perish on the way!"

  He started up, when suddenly a hand
Dropped on his shoulder, and a whisper bland
Said: "My Laodon!" Scarcely spoke, he knew
That gentle voice, and in a moment flew

Into his own Anella's arms, there lay
In speechless rapture, who can e'er portray?
Or give those words in joyful tears impressed,
When words could rise from either blissful breast?
Then, nor till then, the careful maid untied
The full portmanteau lying by her side:
Too well she knew the soldier's sad distress
In wintry camp from want of wholesome dress;
And hence, e'er anxious for her love, she brought
Him garments warm herself had neatly wrought.
Warm is a garb a mother's love returns,
But when a maiden gives it, then it burns;
Through wildest storms, though linen be the dress,
Warmed from the heart that lovèd youth can press.
Such was my sweet Anella's gift:—if aught
In this digression some deem trivial, naught
Will more than it pour balm into the wound
Of those distressed who, like myself, have found
One only friend in this wide world, but she
Was more than all the selfish world to me.
Oh, love! when thou this episode shalt read,
Thy tender tear shall be my priceless meed;
Secure of thee my troubled brow shall rest,
When storms assail me, on thy soothing breast!

    Yet Freedom's cause for those, whose valorous names
Now sleep oblivious, such slight tribute claims.

Laodon and Anella are not new;
Her love, his bravery in hundred view
Who toiled as much, and oft effected more
Than those whose fame stirs every sea and shore;
Whom godlike Washington supremely loved,
As most in Freedom's hour of danger proved.
One such Laodon hurls to endless shame
Lee, Conway, Gates, and all that be the same;
Whom may the Gods in adamantine chains
Bind, that their sprites may never soil our plains!
   But turn thine eye, and pleased behold a Lee
Whose youthful bosom nursed no treachery!
To him, the son of her whose beauty charmed
His youthhood first, our generous leader warmed
With stronger tie, as in those wintry days
The light-horse youth dispersed the foe's forays.
Shame keened their swords, and with two hundred
     strong,
While morn's cold haze enwrapped the hills along,
Sudden upon his scanty force they flew:
He quick into a storehouse near withdrew
His startled braves; thence through the windows
     shed
Such murdering volleys, that the hill o'erspread
With dead and wounded eft th' insulting foe
Shook proudly spurning to the vales below.

Headlong their flight, and with their glittering spoils
Lee soothed the patriots' boreal pains and toils.
His meed to shine as major in the ranks,
But greater prize to gain his general's thanks.
   When now at last the gloomy winter waned,
So often in his slaughtering rage restrained
By him whose tenderness, parental more
Than any sire's, his children's sorrows bore,—
Truth gently scattered envy's discontent,
Broke smoothly off from royalty's battlement
Each frowning rock, and all around earth's sphere
Upraised her champions Freedom's cause to cheer.
Then e'en rebellious chieftains longed to see
Our chief again the leader of the free.
Then rose unfeared from London's senate halls
The dying Chatham's patriotic calls.
From Gallia's schools, no longer duped to bear
Despotic rule, uprose the great Voltaire.
Then Mirabeau humane th' inhuman trade
Of German kinglings like a mountain stayed.
Kant, Lessing spoke philanthropy's sweet praise,
By Goethe, Schiller tuned to silver lays.
Each country longed for despotism's fall,
For Freedom rang from every clime the call;
But to our shores she urged the patriots all.

CANTO VIII.

WHAT heart, or vigorous or worn, but hails
The genial spring, whose tender hand unveils
Earth's fairest beauties from the gelid hue
Of dreary winter to our longing view!
Then fervid youthhood even's balmy hour
Devotes to Venus in the woodbine bower;
Then frosty age unmoved by softer charms
Full in the sun his limbs delighted warms.
All throb with joy, but most those stricken hearts
Whom winter pierced with penury's cold darts;
As were our heroes in the valley drear
With naught but Nature's scanty aids to cheer,
How gleamed their eyes, when from the smouldering
      hearth
Their feet stood warmed upon the green-turfed earth!
Now on the foe! while heaven and earth assist!
For battle's smoke we leave th' encampment's mist;
Nor while we breathe from Freedom's cause desist!
    Yet, gentle spring, ah, why in thy sweet breath
Should hundred lips inhale the bane of death?

And death so cruel, that my spirit reels
In dire alarm, and all my blood congeals!
Fiend, charged by Heaven with hell's malign control!
Again thy fury waked in Brant's fierce soul;
Again thy bastard, Butler, fired his aids
Of lustful Tories on defenceless maids;
Again thy green-clad Johnson stormed to bring
His reeking scalps to Britain's lawless king.
Fair Wyoming! thee threats the bloody storm,
Thee brightly decked in Nature's fairest form;
Laid like a Goddess by that river's side,
Whom, when I first beheld serenely glide
Upon his rocky bed 'tween fields of maize
And pine-topped hills enwrapped in morning's haze,
I thought e'en more delightsome than the stream
Whose murmur first awaked my childish dream.
But why should I attempt to paint thy scene,
Or tell thy human angels, pure, serene?
When gentle Campbell sung thy beauties all,
Thy lovely Gertrude, and thy doleful fall.
My Muse impels me quickly to relate
The ruthless carnage and thy horrid fate.

  As when Helvetia's guileless swains repose
In some green dale that snow-capt Alps inclose,
Sudden a rushing thunder rolls on high:
"Oh, God! the avalanche!" the shepherds cry;

And ere their lips have closed, one horrid pall
Of hugy snow has sepulchred them all:—
Thus suddenly our peaceful Wyoming
Shook with wild yells, and saw all round upspring
Like demons loosened from Tartarean chains,
Relentless savages poured on their plains.
"The Indians!" rang the shriek; but faster far
Rolled on in blood and flames th' inhuman war.
Bent on their plows were laboring farmers crushed;
Their wives and children to their houses rushed,
Pursued as swiftly; wrapt in flames their lives
Paid dire atonement for defrauded knives.
In vain brave Zebulon his yeomen few
Unskilled against the slaughtering squadrons drew;
Like wheat that 'neath the reaper's scythe is cropped
Line after line, heap swelling heap, they dropped
Beneath the stony hatchet and the knife
Whose rage e'en rests not with departed life.
Thus sunk thy last resource, disastrous vale!
If arms oppose not, what can tears avail
Against inhuman foes, who bear no love
Except for blood, nor dread the Powers above?
In woful flight athwart the Mountains Blue
The scattered remnant, wives and children, flew
To where thy patriots, generous Delaware!
Their homesteads with the homeless sufferers share.

While hapless Wyoming, so fair before,
Now lies a waste distained with fire and gore:
Not till nor man nor beast nor house remain
Back to their northern hold withdrew the barbarous
    train.
   Yet think not, savages, no vengeful hand
Will rise in terror on your lawless band!
When shrieks of helpless wives and children rise,
Shall not both tears and wrath inflame the eyes
Of him who bore a father's tender heart
Within a breast no foe's alarm could thwart?
Scarce spring again portentous fates awoke
Than on doomed Seneca the vengeance broke.
Sent by great Washington t' appease the dead
The fiery Sullivan his legion led
Up Susquehanna's mournful vale, still traced
With ashy piles, with clotted gore defaced,
To where the murderers, steeped in revelry,
Enjoyed the spoils of bleeding misery.
They hear th' alarm, their savage war-whoop ring,
Their hatchets lift, and to the combat spring.
Ah, vain your valor fierce! when martial foes,
Not armless yeomanry, their ranks oppose.
Corse stretched on corse they press th' ensanguined
    ground,
The rest fly headlong to the woods around;

Nor there secure; o'er hill, through glen pursued;
With barbarous gore their country lies bestrewed.
One direful waste all Seneca o'erspread,
Like Wyoming, a region of the dead.
Homes smouldering low, fields shorn of wholesome
        grain,
Trees cropped of fruit, e'en grass singed off the
        plain;
All razed whence man his sustenance must gain.
Thus due return for Wyoming was made;—
Sad vengement! yet not else could be delayed
Promiscuous carnage, nor the cruel foe
Be forced to war like men that mercy know.

    But raise thine eyes, and see a nobler feat
Of patriot valor mark the foe's defeat!
Where mighty Hudson rolls his waves betwixt
The rocky Highlands like a rampire fixed
To stay Atlantic's desolating sails
From spreading woe on fair Ontario's vales,
All-potent art, by Washington designed,
Had still more dreadful their resistance lined.
Two frowning cliffs, the eastern Verplanck called,
The western Rockpoint, all approach appalled,
So closely bedded adverse; and when manned
With bristling cannon and a numerous band,
Could baffle siege how well soever planned.

Thus Washington's great scheme;—but scarce a few
Works had been reared, when Albion's war-ships drew
Her mighty legions up the Highland stream,
And for a time delayed the well-planned scheme,
To prosper it the more eftsoons ; for flushed
With momentary victory they rushed
Up the embattled cliffs with all their power,
Filled every rent, and finished every tower.
Both frowned like Gods upon the humbled stream,
Or like those rocks whose adverse bulwarks gleam
On Spain's far strait, by great Alcides reared
As trophies when his barge he thither steered.
But Verplanck Abyla's less grandeur chose ;
Like Calpe unsubdued high Rockpoint rose
In potent majesty : front, either side
Stood proudly washed by Hudson's crystal tide ;
Close to the rear stretched out a deep-sunk fen
O'er which a causeway led for shipless men,
Yet oft laid low beneath the rising flood,
When like a Cyclades the rampire stood.
High parapets and towers the summit crowned,
With mighty culverins close levelled round ;
While midway down the steep declivity
Stretched round the rock two lines of abatis,
Defying more than even walls the foe.
Huge ships of war ploughed thundering below

Six hundred men now formed the guarding band
Obeying Johnson's resolute command.

Meantime great Washington with grief surveyed
His rock-built hope 'neath Britain's talons laid.
" Shall yonder fields, scarce rescued from the foe,
By rampant war again be trodden low ?
Come, daring Wayne ! if fearless deeds thee move, ·
Here is the feat that shall thy courage prove :
This night yon bristling rampire must be ours !
Speak, dar'st thou battle with those vaunting towers ?"
Thus spake the first of chiefs ; to whom replied
The brave whose heart with peril was allied :
" General ! thou know'st from danger ne'er I ran ;
I'll storm e'en hell, if thou but give the plan !"
With pleased affection smiled the godlike chief,
He gave his orders clear, determined, brief ;
Then joined his soldiers camped up near the stream,
While Wayne prepared to execute his scheme.

'Twas at the hour when mortals eased of care
Oblivious slumber's first enjoyment share,
When all is silent save the restless breeze
With rustling forests mingling colloquies,
Or whispering amorous ditties to the stream
Whose crystal eyes with charming rapture gleam ;
Exulting sped along her starry trace
The lovely moon, and with her smiling face

Gazed on three hundred warriors ranged in file
Within grim Dunderberg's close-wedged defile.
For miles unseen, unheard by lurking spy,
Thus far their march had led; now closely nigh
Before them rose the horror-shedding rock,
In ignorance proud defying every shock.
To hurrying feet appeared no easy mound,
Unbarred the waters swept forbidding round.
Yet patriot valor scatters every bar,
Her march triumphant laboring to mar.
Two guards were posted to defend the mound,
At unawares they tumble, gagged and bound.
Swift o'er the flooded causeway stalks along
The line of warriors, eager, bold and strong;
So well observant of their captain's word
To guard sepulchral silence, none yet heard
Of all the foe their coming, still as breath,
But like the kamsin, bearing instant death.

And now the last had crossed the dangerous flood,
And all before the beetling headland stood;
When dauntless Wayne delivered his command,
Dividing right and left his ardent band:
From either flank the bristling cliff to scale,
And joined above bright victory to hail.
Himself the right with gallant Fleury sped,
Stewart and Posey the left column led.

Before them stood the hope-forlorn to rush
First up the rock the abatis to crush:
Twice twenty heroes vowed to death desired,
By Knox and Gibbon brotherly inspired.
Wayne lifts his sword, and like a single man
With levelled bayonets uprolls the van.
No fiery ball they sound to wake the night;
The trenchant steel alone must storm the height.
Thus fought our fathers in those warlike days,
When Gods delighted on their arms to gaze.
The polished greaves their manly legs inclosed,
The golden shield whole clouds of darts opposed,
High on their brows the steely helmet glanced,
Whose sable plumes like war-hawks wildly danced,
Close to their left the brazen falchion hung,
The right hand high the spear chalybean swung.
Oh, Bacon! how Homeric Muses pined
At thy invention never struck thy mind!
Yet it was life's preserver (say the wise),
And for one's life all epics I despise.
On, hope-forlorn! the lower abatis
Sinks 'neath their tread, and onward eagerly
They press upon the upper, when a flash
Darts from above, and rings th' alarming crash.
Quick beat the drums, the warriors fly to arms,
The guns are manned, the volleyed shower warms:

Like hail tempestuous rattling through the sky,
Balls, grape-shot, bomb-shells down the mountain fly;
Like towering maize by driven hailstones torn,
Bends, totters, breaks, and drops the hope-forlorn.
Fifteen among them fall to rise no more,
An equal number welter in their gore.
Impetuous Wayne the singing lead-stone feels
Warmed in his head; he gazes up and reels
In dead-like swoon; two soldiers quickly lend
Their gentle arms, and to his wounds attend.
Eftsoons he waked and cried: "Come, soldiers, bear
Me up the mount; my burial place be there!"
They bore him bravely at his column's head,
A chief who dying still his warriors led.
All Heaven with joy the scene heroic eyed,
And to grim Death at once his prize denied.
On storm the columns, cannon's roaring breath
Returning fast with bayonet's still death.
The walls are reached; the gallant Fleury first
Storms at the gates; asunder wide they burst;
Down sinks the tyrant's flag; bold Posey springs
Upon the gun-decked rampire; wildly rings
The well-proved watchword: "Rockpoint is our own!"
Between their ranks united Britain's groan
Of mad despair arises; not a foe
Escapes to spread their dire defeat below.

But glorious morn beheld our banners gleam
High from the rock above the wondering stream,
Whose kingly ships quaked 'neath Hesperia's hail
So late their own, and turned their tattered sail
Adown the river in disastrous wail.

CANTO IX.

Long had Hesperia borne th' insulting boast
Of Albion's navy prowling round her coast:
When mounts and fields rang far the foe's defeat
Their ocean bulwarks gave a sure retreat,
Whence unawares on some defenceless strand
They dropped anew to ravage all the land.
Hence Falmouth's ashes scattered to the skies,
Long Island's woes, Manhattan's doleful cries,
Penn's godlike city vulgarly profaned,
Savannah's stanch defenders vilely chained.
In conscious might the victors swept along
Our pillaged realms, whose sons, however strong
On field ensanguined, had no ships to brave
The fierce marauders on their sheltered wave.
  But sea, like earth, owns Jove's almighty hand,
And humbly lists his thundering command.
At Alleghania's prayer the blue-eyed Maid,
Whom Heaven empowered our struggling·arms to aid,
Like lightning flew to where Olympus rears
His brow ambrosial 'mid empyreal spheres,

So many glittering messengers to bear
Th' Almighty's orders through the boundless air.
High on a throne of light reclined the God
Who rules all being with his simple nod,
Yet kindly lists to every suppliant's cry,
However lowly; none in vain apply.
But most he loves to grant his heavenly aid
To those who ask him through the blue-eyed Maid;
Whate'er his mind, when she before him prays,
He smiling nods at every word she says.
Thus now Minerva found her heavenly Sire
Against foul Catherine breathing deadly ire,
Who had profaned his shrines with impious thanks
For those who fell in Poland's patriot ranks.
At reverent distance veiled she stood aside
Awaiting his command; he quickly eyed
Her modest form, and: "Come!" he cried; "draw near
To ope thy heart! what wills my daughter dear?"
Eft at his word with soft and gentle tread
The Maiden stepped before his throne and said:

"Almighty Lord of all, to whom alone
Belongs the right to hold a regal throne!
How long shall mortals proud usurp thy right,
Enslaving fellow-men with cruel might?
Thou justly angered gav'st thy heavenly word
Creating equal man, not serf nor lord:

Hesperia first through Despotism's bar
Should break unchecked, and blazon Freedom's star:
Whence guided all should haste Oppression's fall,
And one bright Liberty be shed on all.
Me thou ordain'dst the noble cause to aid;
With joyful heart thy mandate I obeyed.
Nor adverse Fate our valorous arms has checked,
With gorgeous spoils each mount and vale lies decked;
Already Monarchy shakes with alarms,
And Europe's patriots haste to join our arms.
Yet fought in vain our bloody battles seem,
Still insecure our firesides we must deem,
While one vast bulwark unsubdued remains
Whose thunder shatters all our hard-fought gains.
Britannia's war-ships darkening Atlas' waves,
What are his shores but patriots' endless graves?
Can Lincoln's warriors Carolina's coasts
Protect from Arbuthnot's amphibious hosts?
Must thy own son, immortal Washington,
Confined on shore the glorious combat shun,
And ignorant where the dreaded crew may land
Roam sadly pressed along the wasted strand?
Oh suffer not, almighty Sire, such shame
To darken longer Freedom's brilliant name!
Rouse in her sons the Salaminian fire
Which saved all Greece from Persia's potent ire,

And crowd Atlantic with devoted tars
In triumph bearing Appalachia's stars!"
　　She said, and prayingly the Godhead eyed,
Who beaming love affectionately replied :
" Thy words, dear daughter, speak my inmost mind ;
To aid Hesperia's cause I e'er inclined,
Well knowing that of all Tellumo's lands
None more than she will listen my commands.
But toils herculean wait the generous brave
Whom Jove appoints his country's rights to save ;
As none can join these blissful ranks of ours
Unless he fight and crush th' infernal powers.
Thus wills my mind eterne ; and hence the woes
That oft have hindered and will yet oppose
America's bright Freedom ; but the chime
Knolls fast the end of Tyranny's long time.
Thou askest aid to crush th' insulting foe
Whose vaunting sails on every ocean blow :—
Already roused at my command to war
Britannia's prows upsprings the sturdy tar,
Unconquered Jones, by me decreed to grace
The glorious van of that heroic race,
Whose skilful cruisers Albion's flaunting ships
Shall hurl into ignivomous eclipse.
Then rest content : though Fates aversely roll,
E'en they must bend to Jove's supreme control.

Hesperia shall and ever must be free,
Such framed eternally is my decree !"
   Thus spoke the Power, with whose thunder quakes
The solid globe, and heaven's concave shakes.
His blue-eyed daughter reverently withdrew,
All flushed with joy now that his mind she knew;
Till pressing high Olympus' azure bound
She flew adown into the skies profound.
Not half so swiftly on his finny prey
The lordly eagle wings his downward way,
As through the ether star-spangled and blue
The pride of Heaven, fair Minerva, flew.
Italia's vales passed in a moment's glance,
Another viewed the vine-clad hills of France,
The third beheld her touch th' Atlantic beach
Where countless sails in Breton's haven bleach.
Unseen she passed along the crowded strand
To where a captain urged his hardy band
To hurry up a war-ship's deadly freight,
Portentous cannon, charged with lightning fate.
Slim was his frame, his weather-beaten face
Was clouded o'er with melancholy grace;
But from his deep-black eyes incessant fire
Announced the latent hero's fierce desire.
Sudden before him stepped the heavenly Maid,
To him alone revealed, and gently said:

"Illustrious champion! from the realms above
I haste to bring thee Jove's paternal love.
Thee he ordains on Atlas' stormy main
O'er Albion's crew bright victories to gain;
Thy deathless deeds to rouse a sea-bred race
Whose triumphs always Freedom's stars shall grace.
Haste then unfeared t' obey the high decree,
Secure that Jove and Pallas are with thee!"
    To whom the chief, while modestly he eyed
The radiant Goddess, reverently replied:
    "Oh whence this grace, that Jove's supreme delight
Should deign t' appear unto my worthless sight?
I had no titled sires to launch my name
With honors rigged upon the sea of fame.
But what I had wast thou, oh Goddess! me
My heart as to a mother drew to thee.
With thy assistance soon my dauntless hand
On Alfred's deck me gained my first command;
With which to Canso's fishful shoals I steered,
And all his seas from royal pirates cleared.
Thence on swift Ranger's foremast I upraised
My country's flag, the stars and stripes, which gazed
Then first benignly on the joyous wave
That like the sod it fluttered forth to save.
Fast sailed my ship before th' auspicious breeze;
Two brigs I captured in Hibernia's seas,

Another harbored caught my flaming brand
And struck a wreck on Caledonia's strand.
Enraged Britannia's king his war-sloop Drake
Launched forth my cruiser's dreaded force to break.
Off Carrickfergus, where Altantic's tide
Prepares to nestle in the Frith of Clyde,
She hailed us windward; straight my ship I drew
Alongside, challenging her vaunting crew :
'America's ship, Ranger ! we await
Your twenty guns. Come on ! The hour is late.'
And instantly our eighteen guns oped wide
Their roaring lips; the foe as quick replied.
One murderous hour the sulphurous eclipse
Hung black between the fulminating ships;
When struck the Briton's flag, and silence dull
Revealed her battered sails, her shattered hull,
Her captain and twice twenty of her crew
Laid cold in death. The piteous wreck we drew
Safe to this shore; whence I again prepare
At Heaven's command our ocean foe to dare."
   He ceased; the Goddess with the azure eyes
Benignly smiled, then vanished in the skies.
Jones rigged his vessel, vowed to Heaven's Maid
With her own name, and gayly anchor weighed.
Propitious gales her scudding swiftly bore
Round Britain's isles to Flamboro's high shore.

Softly the moon her silver lustre shed
On England's sea that like a mirror spread
Blue and serene beneath the promont's head
Sudden to south a war-decked cruiser loomed
Full under lee, and like a tempest boomed
Against Hesperia's war-ship. She intent
Stood firmly swayed, a sea-built battlement.
Up bore the foe, her streaming flag displayed,
And hailed defiantly the God-sprung Maid:
"Serapis comes thy rebel flag to bring
An easy trophy to Britannia's king!"
"If hard or easy," valiant Jones replied,
"My Goddess-favored ship shall soon decide!"
And tacking round her murdering guns he brings
Full on the foe-ship's larboard hull, and flings
The fiery shot into her riven side.—
But hark! a fearful crash bursts scattering wide
With mangled corses fair Minerva's deck!
Oh compound terrible! what power can check
Thy blinded fury, when the war-tube's sides,
Some part neglected, thy swift flash divides?
In rush the waves, the lower ports are closed;
With still less guns, less men must be opposed
The foe, who conscious of their power burn
With ardor fierce, and deadly shots return
To weakened volleys. Yet untouched by fears
To windward Jones his battered vessel steers.

And as the lion, when assailed afar
With showers of darts in ignominious war
He must succumb ere long, this kenned o'erleaps
The dangerous barrier, and resistless sweeps
His boasting foes to earth, a helpless deer
When fought afar, the lord of beasts when near:
So while at distance Albion's fire must rake
His riddled hull and all resistance break,
Our captain, known the power of his band
When grappling close they battle hand to hand,
Unfurls each sail, bids every rudder ply
To cross the clouded space, till grimly nigh
Hull pressed to hull conjoins the hostile ships
And adverse cannon kiss each other's lips.
Swift at his captain's word the gallant Dale
Tugs at the jib-stay of Serapis' sail,
And with strong cables binds it deadly fast
To bright Minerva's towering mizzen-mast.

Proud Pearson wonder-struck the grapple eyed,
Yet gibed his foe with wonted British pride:
"Has Pallas struck?" To whom our chief incensed:
"Cease prattling, till the fight I have commenced!"
Loud cheered his tars, the bugle briskly played,
And instantly a murdering hand-grenade
Shot from Minerva's topmast whizzing sped
Upon Serapis' deck, burst wide, and spread

Grim-mangled death with its dissevered shell;
While hissing round its blazing kernel fell
Into the heaped up cartridges that loud
Exploding swelled still more the slaughtered crowd.
Death, how terrific is thy bloody sway
When uncontrolled thou mixest in the fray!
Here viscid brains from battered foreheads rush,
There entrails foul from ripped abdomens gush;
A tar, both legs cut off, here gasping lies,
Another arms bereft there piteous cries;
No tender hand consoles the dying brave,
Far, far from home he sinks into the wave.
Ah, foe! how I condole with thee, and more
Because for Tyranny thou shedd'st thy gore!
Lo! undismayed the brave survivors spurn
Grim slaughter's rage, and to their guns return.
Fiercely along the close-linked starboards glares
The ceaseless flash, the short-cut thunder tears
Enraged the iron-plated planks, or chides
His loaded rival in his brazen sides.
Out burst the flames and wrap in sheeted fire
The shattered hulls, thence to the rigging spire
In lightning blaze; and yet the conflict burns
E'en more inflamed—till England's crew returns
A feeble fire, then strikes the burning sail.
Their humbled Pearson by our valorous Dale

Is led a captive from Serapis' wreck
To meet the victor on Minerva's deck.
He generously his hard-fought triumph bears,
Subdues the flames, his battered ship repairs,
And through the channel tugs his prize, while thrones
Gaze trembling on and dread the power of Jones.

CANTO X.

ATHWART Atlantic trembling with the fire
Of Gaul and Briton met in hostile ire
My Muse transports me to yon azure mounts
Whose snowy crests yield substance to the founts
Of Yadkin lost in conquering Pedee,
Catawba, Broad, Saluda, Congaree
Blue Ocean greeting through the great Santee.
Deep lie the fertile valleys wedged between
High ridgy forests clad in fadeless green.
Along the streams that icy springs supply
Vast herds of cattle on the greensward lie,
Whose swains like patriarchs of the olden times
Rule independently these genial climes,
Or like those warriors whom Pelayo's sword
Roused in Asturia 'gainst Almanzor's horde:
The Mountain Men of Carolina, reared
In mutual league, by every foeman feared;
Called any moment by the clang of war
At once they meet from holds however far,
Steal Indian-like the bushy brakes between
And fire upon the foe from points unseen;

Who less or more in numbers eft must fall
Beneath a power whose swiftness baffles all
Approach, and whom though checked no dire defeats
    appall.
   Thus often roused at Liberty's command
Again now met the hardy mountain band.
Fierce Ferguson, with royal hate imbued,
Through Carolina's rice-clad fields pursued
His patriot victims.   Waste and slaughter spread
Her cedar-lawns with fire and mangled dead.
Already Appalachia's mountains shook
With dire alarm, and cast a praying look;
When peal on peal the highland bugle rung,
The forests quivered, from each glen upsprung
The mounted warrior, met another, third,
Scores, each a brother, all united spurred
To Gilbert's hamlet, where from every side
In poured the mountains' self-impelling tide.
First gallant Clarke with Georgia's sons appeared,
Next Williams Granville's hardy yeomen cheered.
Boone urged Kentucky's wild and furious sons
Like Indians decked with furs and moggasons.
With Sevier and with Shelby Tennessee
From Holston's banks sent forth her cavalry.
By Dowell bold and prudent Cleveland led
Were Rutherford's and Surrey's warriors sped.

Last, but not least, from distant Powell came
The dauntless Campbell of undying fame.
Him, having farthest come, the mountain band
Select at once to take the chief command
Republican, not regal; each obeys
His nearest captain, or his own best ways.
Three thousand thus pant for the coming fight,
A motley host, but dreadful to the sight:
Some like Hesperian soldiers dressed in blue,
Others in homespun garbs of grizzly hue;
But most preferred the dress of backwood Boone,
The Indian shirt and greave and gaudy shoon.
Most rode their steeds; when summoned to the fray
Their order was: seize gun, mount, dash away!
When nigh the foe, their steeds apart they drew
Them fastening to the trees, on foot then flew
Into the combat; if o'erpowered, away
On nimble horse; if victors, no delay
With clattering hoof to take the fleeing prey.
   Such were the rough-trained warriors gathered
      round
The cots of Gilbert on the swarded ground.
Meanwhile, ere blow the bugle's warlike blast,
They form in groups to share the crude repast.
Part from the herd that grazes near select
The fattest steer, their levelled tubes direct

Full at his forehead—click! the ball him knocks,
And to the ground loud bellowing falls the ox.
Straight through his throat the ready knife is drawn,
His smoking gore spouts on the grassy lawn.
Gasping he dies : the soldiers loose his hide,
The foul cast off, the chosen parts divide
In equal shares.   Each turns with soldier art
Above the blazing fire his spitted part;
Then to their lips the roasted beef they bring,
And slake their thirst with water from the spring.
Nor social talk is banished their regale;
Each has a question, each a stirring tale.
But all attend, when Williams asks to know
Of posted Campbell what of Northern foe.
They press around, in front, on side, behind
The bold Virginian, who thus speaks his mind:
   "Could dark oblivion hide ignoble fame,
To what more welcome than a traitor's name!
Then from my lips a tale should never fall
Whose blackness every patriot must appall.
Yet what swift Fame eftsoons will spread, as well
I now, however sad the task, may tell.
Who would have thought the soldier, whom could check
No northern wilds, who under steep Quebec
Bled for his country, who from Schuyler's wall
Drove Leger's legions, who at Freedom's call,

Unheeding envious Gates, stormed Burgoyne's camp,
Where gallant Frazer, charging down the champ
On iron-gray, embraced the field of gore,
And Breymann, once saved, fell to rise no more,—
Himself a cripple borne from off the plain,
Struck in that blessed member once again;—
Him—aye ye quiver with disdain!—yet he
Now reaps in Britain's ranks his dastard treachery!
Foiled in ambitious schemes by tongues ingrate
To valor all must own, a demon's hate
Impelled his soul to seek with artful wiles
The first command of Hudson's walled defiles.
That gained, at once the hellish scheme he planned
To ope his trust to Clinton's leaguering band.
A youth there was then, Andre called, the same
Who had illumed proud Howe's ignoble name;
A lovesick rhymester, fitted less to share
The battle's din than concerts of the fair;
Yet prized by British chiefs for wily art,
And well disposed to act a spy's black part.
Him Clinton chose the traitor chief to meet·
And seal with him Ontario's dire defeat.
Where Hudson groans in Clove's high-frowning shade,
The owl and whippoorwill the day evade,
And serpents revel,—dreading still the light
The pair accursèd meet in dead of night.

The kiss is given: north the traitor speeds;
The Briton o'er Manhattan's neutral meads
With fearful heart spurs south, where Albion rears
Her bristling battlements. Nor vain his fears!
For sudden, coming to a stream that fell
Athwart his path pressed in a woody dell,
Three soldiers dressed in garb of refugees
With levelled muskets sprang from out the trees
Him thundering to stand. Their dress deceived
The timid youth. Of proper garb bereaved
In British dungeons by a cruel foe
They had no other. 'Soldiers, from below,
I hope, your party hails, as I do!' cried
The Briton. 'Thou think'st rightly!' they replied.
Joy unreserved lit Andre's face; he spoke
His office and some errands false; then took
The golden horologe from out his vest,
Which undeniably his worth confessed.
Too confident young heart! with startled ears
The words: 'We are Americans!' he hears;
'Thou art our prisoner!' In vain his wiles
Now tempt a patriot's unaffected smiles.
'Dismount!' they cry; his charger's reins they seize;
One, Williams, guides the horse, while to the trees
Beside the stream Van Wart and Paulding lead
The struggling captive vainly threat or meed

Presenting. Quick the search begins. The round
Small hat, the blue surtout, the red coat bound
With golden lace, the nankin vest, all show
No sinister design ; to let him go
Already they intend, when Paulding cries :
' Off with his boots !' and Andre's eyes
Turn wildly round. All now is lost ! there lie
The traitor's charts. 'Ye Gods ! he is a spy !'
Exclaim the patriots. 'Tis enough, though more
They could not then divine, and eft before
The chief of men their captive strange they led.
Ah ! who can feel what ravenous vultures fed
Upon the traitor's heart, when that keen eye
To all the world revealed his treachery ?
Yet, blessed be Jove ! the dastard scheme was crushed
While still no foe in wily triumph flushed.
To Britain's ranks the cursed traitor fled,
Whence now against the land for which he bled
He pants to battle at the Tories' head.
But Andre, tried and sentenced as a spy,
Though foe and friend by pity led awry
Besought to spare his youth, that hardest doom
Was forced to meet, the gibbet's shameful tomb."

Here Campbell ceased, and thoughtful silence held
Each breast inthralled, by Shelby thus dispelled :
" Whate'er a spy from war-courts may await,
Young Andre seems deserved of milder fate.

The traitor's doom no pity ever claimed;
Him could we seize, the leg for Freedom maimed
We would cut off and give a soldier's grave;
The vile remains should on the gallows quave.
But Andre young, by royal zeal misled,
This joy gives only that one foe is dead."

  " My brother-chief !" Virginia's son replied;
" Judge not ere truth show thee another side !
A much-loved friend I had, his name was Hale,
For years my classmate in the schools of Yale,
Young, ardent, handsome, skilled alike to gain
Fame on Parnassus or on Mars's plain.
His country's voice the latter claimed; beneath
Bostonia's walls he reaped a chieftain's wreath:
Thence on Long Island fought with vigorous hand,
First to return to that disastrous strand.
For godlike Washington desired to know
The site and strength of his embattled foe.
His wish no sooner kenned, than ardent Hale
Asked for the post from which the boldest quail.
Not reckless daring, but pure patriot love
Impelled his soul the perils sure to prove.
Disguised as pedagogue he crossed the Sound
In dead of night, and reached the battle-ground;
Surveyed th' encampments with suspectless view,
Of towers and trenches noted figures drew,

Which having hidden in his shoon, he sought
Again the boat which thither had him brought.
A boat indeed he found there drawn to shore,
And hastened toward it, when—upsprang before
His startled gaze the unsuspected crew,
Britannia's hirelings, and their muskets drew
Straight at his breast;—no succoring arm was nigh;—
Like Andre searched he proved a hopeless spy.
Brought to Manhattan while the wasteful fire,
By patriots thought ignited, Howe's rash ire
Incensed to rage, the noble captive's fate
Was quickly sealed by Britain's wonted hate.
Like Andre he was hanged, but tenderness
Was ever shown to that, while cruelness
Embittered this one's pangs unto the last.
By Cunningham, the brutal provost, cast
Into a loathsome den, when he desired
That saintly Writ by Heaven's Love inspired,
It was refused; when to a mother's heart
He had penned down those feelings which impart
Such consolations dear to whom behind
We leave, e'en they were scattered to the wind,
' Those rebels ne'er shall know,' the hangman cried,
' They had a man who with such firmness died !'
Firmly, forsooth, he braved untimely death,
His patriot soul fled with his dying breath:

' My only sorrow, that I cannot prove
With more than this lost life my country's love !'
Immortal Hale ! may we——"

                        Hark ! sounds the tramp
Of clattering chargers toward the startled camp.
The bugle shrills—a moment—and before
Them spur two horsemen soiled with mire and gore.
" The foe is near !" they gasp, " a scouting band
Came on our track and shouted us to stand.
We off in headlong gallop, while around
Our heads their grape-shot whistled ; to the ground
Dropped Locke and Graham ; we alone got clear,
Though wounded sore ; but soon they must be here !"

    "On, boys !" cried Campbell ; " not a moment's rest,
Till we burn out this robber's Tory nest !"
Some foelike troopers on the mounts appear,
But dash away as fast o'erwhelmed with fear.
Wild shouts of glee from every patriot rise,
Each lifts his gun, and on his war-horse flies.
Away they go, no urger they require,
Hale's dying words their noble breasts inspire,
And comrades slain rouse vengement's fierce desire.
What host must not to such an army yield,
Where each a hero rushes to the field !
Such were the braves who at Thermopylæ
Saved Græcia's realms from Persia's tyranny.

Such were the Romans, when a Cocles fought
Before the crumbling bridge, and Mucius sought
Etruria's despot in his tent, and turned
Destruction's legions with his right hand burned.
Such later still the bold Batavians were,
When patriot Haring all alone could dare
Fierce Alva's thousand on the Diemer-mound,
Till, safe his comrades all, he swam the blood-dyed
     sound.
Such—but enough ! why foreign virtue trace,
When all her charms our native heroes grace ?
These, Alleghania, are thy fondest theme,
With them I spur o'er Broad's rock-bedded stream,
And pant to see bright triumph on them gleam !

CANTO XI.

High o'er his brethren, who appalled have fled
To heights less terrible, his massive head
King's Mount uplifts to Carolina's sky,
Whose philters yet his blandishments deny,
His name abhorring.   But the tyrant's crew
At once his title and his grandeur drew.
Precipitous the rear, but either side
And front declivous to the swale subside.
The lofty pines of tangled brushwood freed
Give plenteous space unto the scampering steed ;
While interspersed huge rocks of grayish hue
The deadly marksman screen from hostile view.
A level ridge the frowning summit forms,
That seems to smile at warfare's gathering storms.
On this proud Ferguson had ranged his band,
And while he eyed his stronghold high his hand
He raised in fierce defiance : " Hence, though hell
Her rebels all should on our ranks impel,
They never could our bristling arms repel !"
   Him boasting thus Hesperia's sons beheld
As toward the mount their swift pursuit they held.

Near by a streamlet pierces the ravine,
Whose rugged sides close-planted cedars screen;
There each dismounts and ties his panting steed
As erst secured to trunk or branch or reed.
Then drawing near, the war-charged mount to storm
From either flank and in the front, they form
In three divisions.   That which frontward speeds
With gallant Shelby fearless Campbell leads.
Williams and Cleveland urge the left to fight,
While Sevier guides with Dowell's aid the right.
The mountain's base is reached; awhile they stand
Intent to hear their chieftain's brief command.
How different from warfare's studied art,
Where head usurps the office of the heart,
And each scared fool stuck on a hill afar
With chart and spy-glass may direct the war!
America's first champions little said,
They made their muskets answer in their stead;
Their chiefs were only to conduct the way
In face of danger to the deadliest fray.
Thus Champbell. "Onward now, my men!" he cried;
"When up the mount, each for himself decide
Where best and fastest can his rifle fire,
Now to press on, then for awhile retire
Behind a tree or rock, but never leave
The battle-field, till triumph we achieve!"

From thrice ten hundred breasts the brave reply
Rings to his words: "To conquer or to die!"
The flank-assailing columns press to gain
Their stations marked, while those in front remain
Bent on the signal. It is given. Quick
As strikes the flint upon the gunlock's click,
Or as upon the lyric master's "Three"
Upswells the well-directed melody,
Moves and uprises at the word of fight
Our patriot host against th' embattled height.
And as up Penn's steep cliff the iron-horse
Swift rushing yet exerts such equal force
That in the night the rider scarce can know
He mounts a steep·with yawning dells below,
So steady and with spirits naught can quail
The bold Hesperians up the mountain scale.
Grim Ferguson awaits them in his lair
As longs a vulture for the timid hare,
When unsuspecting up the hill he skims,
Nor heeds the shadow that the daylight dims,
To him disastrous; not to valorous hearts
Who ken their foe, his courage, force, and arts.
    Two hours of light yet promised Circe's sire,
When Williams oped the rifle's fatal fire
Which Albion's left advance with slaughter strewed
And toward the ridge the scattered rest pursued.

Round Ferguson him turned—when all the brunt
Of hissing onset rattles in his front.
There Campbell stands, a foe none may despise;
He wheels around and furious on him flies.
Full hundred guns their whistling lead-stones send—
In idle air; for quick the patriots bend
Behind the trees and rocks; thence all concealed
Their certain fire hurl on the foe revealed.
"On with your bayonets!" the Briton cries;
"Clear every nook that open war defies!"
They rush adown, but while the front they scour
Upon their right reopes another shower
From Sevier's band; when turning round on this
From front renewed and left new volleys hiss.
As when in Seville's wide arena stands
The forest-monarch, while the conynge hands
Of matadores their scarlet mantles wave
That make his furious brain more wildly rave,
At last he fixes on one daring foe,
Prepares his horn and darts to give the blow;
Sudden he feels a shaft his flanks transpierce,
At once he turns now more than ever fierce
On this new foe, but ere the thrust is given
Another goads him off—till madly driven
By dart and cloak and his own spouting gore
He sinks beneath the slaying matadore:

So dauntless Ferguson in vain essays
New sallies to and fro, they only raise
Fresh foes on right and left, in front and rear;
Oft though repulsed as oft they reappear
Checked but unconquered, while his fearless band
Fall fast and thick upon the gravelly sand.
Yet on he battles, till the rifle's breath
Whirls through his brain the singing globe of death;
His swimming eyes turn in their sockets round,
He reels and droops and thunders to the ground;
His white horse, checked no more, the rein denies,
Snorts terror-struck and down the mountain flies.

This closed the bloody fray; the chiefless band,
Eight hundred left, sought Mercy's generous hand
Thrice hundred of their comrades lay around
In painless death or writhing with the wound.
Of Freedom's sons twice ten had purpled o'er
The mount contested with their sacred gore.
Among whom Williams rent with gashes lay,
The first to tempt and perish in the fray;
How changed, alas! since that eventful hour!
Gone were those terrors which had forced to cower
The boldest foe; his features pale and cold
Naught but the joy which death procured him told.
All mourned his fate, for he was brave and good;
But none bewailed like him who aye had stood

In weal and woe a comrade by his side,
And who now longed he there with him had died.
E'en when Apollo had reposed his car
To take his couch in Aphrodite's star,
True Campbell o'er the corse endearèd bent,
Effused his tear and moaned his sore lament—
Till overpowered with weariness and grief
He sought in sleep a momently relief.

 Kind son of Erebus, when was thy share,
Though e'er so sweet to hearts oppressed with care,
To dearer object than to this assigned,
Where o'er his slaughtered friend the chief reclined !
Soft be thy balm where Venus spreads her bower,
As when of yore the cloud-compelling Power
On Ida's summit with fair Juno lay ;
Yet such may taste their joys in open day :
But when the heart is plunged in sorrows deep,
Then thou art needed, or we perish, Sleep !
Then eke to thee our heartiest thanks arise,
Because thou givest what all else denies.
Such was thy gift to yon deep-wounded breast,
Which then at least lay soothed in balmy rest.
He thought not, felt not, knew not that he lay
Upon a form now more than ever—clay ;
He saw not how above him brightly shone
The bickering gems of Jove's cerulean throne ;

He heard not eager hawks scream o'er their prey,
Nor hungry dogs drag shattered skulls away;
All dark below, above all heavenly fair:
Such is too oft the noble heart's black share;
Who be the cause, let wiser lips declare!

I have not labored to bring on a doom
Which makes me wander in continual gloom;
I have abhorred this selfish world, 'tis true,
And shall do so forever, nor can rue
The bitter scorn with which I have repaid
Hypocrisy's deceits; but I have made
No kind heart grieve, and yet in thankless meed
My own has often been compelled to bleed.
Be it continued! if my youth so far
Has borne the brunt, I can sustain the war.

Thrice-happy sleeper! whom at least awhile
Sweet dreams of love and glory can beguile.
Are thine such, hero! or doth martial strife
Thee awake anew to this our bitter life?
What heats his forehead? makes his bosom heave?
Clinch tight his sword, as if he sought to cleave
A Briton's head? His mind on some far plain
Must roam, or wander o'er this mount again.
Thou, Morpheus, whom thy father, Sleep, of all
Loves most, my Campbell's wondrous dream recall!

Dreams oft expose the hidden web of Fate,
And we must humbly their event await.

On that high mound which rises from the meads
Whose far-stretched clover Hannah's cattle feeds,
Near which the Broad meandering sheds his flood
Of wholesome waters, it appeared he stood
All ready to receive the dreaded foe
Whose numerous war-steeds pawed the plain below
High soared their hopes, as gayly at their head
Rode fearless Tarleton, Carolina's dread;
He who alone her Bayard unsubdued
Into his dankest marshes had pursued,
And, though the Fox could never be ensnared,
Had most her fields with ruthless ravage shared.
Again his former comrades gathered round
Our dreaming hero on th' embattled mound,
With other chieftains added to their band
From nigh and far 'neath Morgan's first command:
Call, Pickens, Howard, and the youth whose name
Did not obscure a Washington's bright fame.
Not long such ardent foes inactive wait,
They rush ahead preventing tardy Fate
And ending fast their feuds inveterate.

As when a pack of noisy curs invade
A herd of cattle browsing in the glade,

Their yelping cries the timid kine affright
Who stretching tail start off in jingling flight;
Not so the bulls; they stand with lordly scorn,
Their broad heads lower and point the sturdy horn;
Wo him whom rashness tempts that front to dare!
Gored through his bowels he's tossed into the air;
Their dauntless valor makes the females burn
With honest shame, their hanging foes they spurn
From off their haunches, strike and toss around
Till not a cur but whines upon the ground:—
Thus, if with great small things may be compared,
The scene of raging war at first appeared
On yon embattled height; but diffcrent far,
As planet real is from apparent star,
Was Morgan's mind from his dissenting hand;
Shock, feinted flight, return all his command.
When at the foe's first charge fell back our ranks,
It was but to assail his guardless flanks
With other troops; whence some like cowards ap-
     peared,
Like heroes others; but not one there feared
Th' impetuous foe: in the retreaters rushed,
And from all sides the British lines were crushed.
In vain to rally them fierce Tarleton strove,
In vain his reckless oaths at partial Jove;

The Thunderer smote him with eterne disgrace,
Such as attends the coward's dastard chase:
While hundred Britons stayed to rise no more,
And twice as many weltered in their gore.
But of yon fifty, who to freedom gave
Their sacred blood, twelve shared that honored grave,
Which Gods bestow on every patriot brave:
Th' Elysian fields, where heavenly maids caress
Their splendent wounds, and every pang redress.

Again the sleeping hero thought he stood
On Mars's field, but now by Eutaw's flood;
Where gallant Greene, great Washington's loved son,
O'er Stuart's host unfaded laurels won;
Which like the olive-branch from Noah's ark
From all the South dispelled the cheerless dark.
This Campbell saw, but eke his piercing eyes
Beheld by Fate foredoomed the dear-bought prize:
How at his general's order, first to pour
The deadly volley and then rush to scour
With levelled bayonet the foe-thronged field,
His bold Virginians never known to yield
He hurried on; black rose the murdering dust,
And through it gleamed prepared to give the thrust
The fixèd steel; down horse and rider came
In carnage mingled wild;—but lo! a flame

His clicking herald speeds; and at the sound
The wounded patriot falls unto the ground.
Yet conscience fails not; with his right hand pressed
Upon his gun, and on his deep-gashed breast
His left, he eyes and lists the raging war
Now o'er him, then beside him, near, afar,
Then asks a comrade: "Who is it that flies?"
"The foe!" is answered; and the hero cries:
"I die contented!"———

        Starts the dreaming chief
Waked by the struggle, and renews his grief
O'er Williams cold below, himself alive
Forced still alone with toilsome breath to strive.
"Oh, that my dream were truth!" he longing cries;
"Eftsoons it will!" an inward God replies.

CANTO XII.

Guide of my steps, Hesperian Muse! although
With Halleck, Whittier, Bryant, Longfellow,
Thy chosen sons, my name can never rhyme,
Yet I have loved thee, even when a crime
This was reputed, on thy charmful mount
Have lingered long to sip thy sacred fount,
And when thou gavest me thy loving hand,
Have not disowned thee in my native land.
Such I have been; I speak not to upbraid—
Ye Gods attest!—for what to heavenly Maid
Compared is man? but only I desire
For this my love some of that living fire,
With which burned he who raised to deathless fame
The great Achilles; shall not equal flame
Inspire the bard at Washington's bright name?

On York's south shore, where first the Ocean Bay
The widening river hails at distance, lay
Encamped the remnant of that mighty host
Who had so long despoiled the South's fair coast.
Now dwindled scarce by battles long and fierce
They bravely strove Virginia's wilds to pierce,

And join their comrades in Manhattan's walls
Ere Fate reversed should whelm them in her squalls.
All vain-thought schemes; scarce had their wayworn
    band
Reposed a moment on this fatal strand,
Than sudden dangers rose on every side :
Before, behind them, on their right the tide
Of York and James and blue Atlantic bore
The hostile fleet of thousands to their shore.
Upon their left, the only passage where
On solid earth a sally they could dare,
Appeared with legions thwarting all escape
The godlike chief in formidable shape.
Thus 'mid Phthiotis' valiant warriors stood
The son of Peleus by Scamander's flood;
So great the terror which before him swept,
That hundred Trojans frantic-driven leaped
Into the gory stream, preferring death
In piteous wave to that unsparing breath.
Not less the sight of Liberty's right arm
The whelps of Tyranny shook with alarm;
Far more inviting seemed the surging wave
Than boldly faced that frowing front to brave;
Yet here, proud Despotism, shall be dug thy grave !
    Immortal heroes, who for freeborn peace
Have fought thus far, here eke your labors cease !

Rise, bleeding shades, by glorious Parker led,
And here behold for what your hearts have bled !
Gaze on the kindling eye of yonder sage,
And read Hesperia's happy future age !
Rapt into hidden lore the bardic seer
Eyes Freedom conquering the world appear :
Cornwallis humbled, eft Britannia's king
Hastes Independence to our realms to bring.
To thirteen States new provinces accede,
All held by people from Oppression freed.
Vermont thus first augments the Ten and Three,
Kentucky next and mountain Tennessee ;
Ohio then her wood-crowned hillocks joins,
While Indiana girds her blooming loins
With Liberty's striped flag, and from her plains
The mighty sister, Illinois, unchains.
Along the Gulf her boundless cotton fields
With Alabama Mississippi yields ;
Hastes Florida, and Louisiana brings
The floated wealth of great Missouri's springs.
Arkansas, tarry not, nor, Tahlequah !
Lo ! how the frigid North begins to thaw !
With Michigan's and bleak Wisconsin's breaks
Th' enslaver's ice from Minnesota's lakes ;
Hears Iowa and on Missouri calls
To free their forests from Oppression's thralls.

The South-West wears impatiently her bands
Till Texas opes her mighty table-lands,
And Mexico and Arizona show
With honest pride their mounts of freeborn snow.
"What! I behind!" shouts Kansas from her plains;
Nebraska joins, Dakota not refrains.
Montana's woodlands and Nevada's fields
Haste to produce what peopled Utah yields;
Nor Idaho's and Colorado's gold
The Indian sprites from Freedom's sons withhold.
Last, though not least, by piny Oregon
His province finds the godlike Washington;
While California like Ontario pours
O'er boundless Ocean her exhaustless stores.
    But can a region of such vast extent
Possess a spirit on one purpose bent?
Dawns not the day, when freemen led awry
By lucre's bane shall raise Secession's cry?
And must we see our happy fields imbrued
With blood fraternal hot from deadly feud?
Oh, speak not thus, all-seeing bard! but close
My weeping eyes on such unmeasured woes!
Depart, ye shades! in vain your hearts have bled;
Go, and me number with the happy dead!
But lo! the cloud has disappeared, and bright
As ne'er before my country greets my sight.

12

Then, brothers, list our slaughtered chieftain's call,
With Mercy's balm to soothe Rebellion's fall!
He was so kind; who ever called in vain
Upon that heart? to ask was to obtain.
Be he our model! and like Romans show,
We war the proud, but spare the fallen foe!
With North let South send forth her daughters fair,
And o'er his grave their unison declare;
That future bards may kindle at the name
Of generous Lincoln, and his spotless fame
With that of Washington to endless age proclaim!

All this announced the heaven-inspirèd seer,
And still new wonders in his eyes appear.
Warmed at Hesperia's undissevered force,
See Freedom rise and claim a wider course!
How sinks the son of Hapsburg's haughty line,
Who sought a crown at Montezuma's shrine;
How Erin's sons shake Albion's tottering throne
So long impervious to her piteous groan;
How Brutus fires in Garibaldi's breast
That love of Liberty so long depressed:
Hail, Cicero! hail, all ye Fabii! come,
Once more to live in liberated Rome!
Enlightened Freedom every breast inspires,
Before her blaze dark Tyranny expires.
On, patriots! strike, until the last king's head
Is ground to dust beneath your freeing tread!

Then shall the golden age of Liberty
Proclaim all earth the home of brave and free !
  What thus Hesperian spirits then beheld
Was not, methinks, from their first chief withheld.
How glowed his brow, as o'er the leaguered town
Which held the remnant of that host, whose frown
So long had dimmed his country's brightest hope,
He shot the glances of his telescope !
It told him all their desperate alarm ;
And yet cold thought that brow with rapture warm
Lined with her furrows, as if Fate awhile
Gleamed promising, and then withheld her smile.
  As when the hunter many a weary day
Has through the woods pursued his fleet-foot prey,
And oft already has the net been spread,
And oft the feathered arrow has been sped,
Yet that has snapped and this its course has left—
Till blindly rushing through a narrow cleft
Of rocks precipitous closed in the rear
Pants terror-struck the hope-bereavèd deer ;
Then though the huntsman all escape excludes
He more than ever hasty zeal precludes,
Stung by the failure of his former toil
And keened by sight of overcertain spoil :
Thus prudent Washington, so long distressed
By hundred schemes that never promised rest,

Now that they all had centred on this spot,
And promise gave of Freedom's happy lot
Fixed and immovable, yet all aware
Of Fortune's fickleness, his wonted care
E'en more than ever now increased, and wrought
Such meshy toils around his foe, that nought
To leaguered Britain seemed to ope release,
Whom hostile land inclosed and more than hostile
    seas.

    As when a troop of foresters and hounds
The boar couched 'mid his family surrounds,
Fiercely he starts up from his smoking lair,
Grunts, grinds his tusks, and rears his bristling hair;
His mate him seconds with her fearless young—
A moment—and the tusky race has sprung
This way and that upon the armèd foe,
Each willing certain death to share, that so
Some may escape the common-levelled blow:
Thus when Cornwallis every outlet round
Of land or water foe-embattled found,
His British pride waxed desperately fierce,
And "or to die or through yon barriers pierce"
His only watchword; like devotion grew
In all his Britons and them round him drew.
Four ships of sail and sixteen urged by oar
Still rode protected by their northern shore,

In which, while part of their devoted band
Would brave the terrors of the foe on land,
The rest enshrouded in the mists of night
Athwart the river might secure their flight.

Ill-fated chief! how vanishes thy scheme,
Like skimming pebble in the circling stream!
Lo! springs a mound, that bristling cannon crown,
Six hundred yards scarce distant from the town,
And o'er it high with fixed and threatening hand
The first of chieftains swings the lighted brand;
Portentous signal! whence with pealing din
First "Union" flashes, then each culverin
Spouts forth the bomb-shell or the solid ball
United crashing on the crumbling wall.
Yet Britain sinks not like a timid deer,
But like a lion, when his foemen near
His den surround him, she prepares to fling
In fierce return her equal thundering.
Incessant balls each other cross in air,
Strike to the ground and furrowing uptear
The smoking glebe, or soaring onward leap
Into the stream, like monsters of the deep
Upspouting high and far the dashing spray.
Black was their passage through the sultry day,
Like spectres darting 'twixt the volumes dun
Of sulphurous clouds that hid the fiery sun.

But through the night with meteoric glare
Like blazing comets they illumed the air.
Then soared the bomb-shell like a rocket high,
But not to grace the inoffensive sky,
For lowering down upon the wall it fell
With dreadful crash, and from the bursted shell
The loosened earth-stars flew, that widely spread
Rocks, glaring rubbish, arms and mangled dead.

 Six days and nights thus raged the fiery showers,
Each blast reducing Albion's stately towers;
Her ships of sail by flaming meteors riven
And o'er the stream in thousand fragments driven;
Her strong redoubts, that rising in her front
Had from her rampires shaken battle's brunt,
In one fierce night by Hamilton's bold band
Secured a bulwark to the foe's command.
And now already stares into her face
The cannon's range athwart the narrow space
Of but three hundred ells; with lorded scope
To certain death their fuming lips they ope;
No airy foe disputes their fiery path,
The last has withered 'neath their breath of wrath.

 Yet fertile Hope espies a glimmering light
From base surrender in less shameful flight.
The sixteen boats are manned to row them o'er
York's gulfy stream to Gloucester's saving shore.

Night aids their scheme, already midway ply
The labored oars, when suddenly the sky
Shows dire portents : fierce Caurus madly roars
Athwart the billowy river and outpours
Whole clouds of rain, while Jove's fulmineous light
To keen Hesperia opes their hurried flight.
Out flash her guns ; by earth and heaven driven
Adown the stream, dispersed, upset and riven
None of their boats secure the destined shore ;
Few saved from wreckage bends the shattered oar
To York's disastrous strand, the only spot
Which Fates averse still to their feet allot,
Yet but a target for the cannon's murdering shot.
　　Here sink their hopes ; they pray our raking fire
To cease, and listen to their last desire:
"Be yours in peace the hard-contested field,
Our arms and all to you we humbly yield,
But spare our lives !" We proffer them our hand
In sacred trust to keep their low demand.
Then slowly moving in funereal train
Six thousand Britons issue on the plain,
And while with shouldered guns we stand around
They fast and sullenly their muskets ground :
Last din of tyrant arms on Freedom's shore,
So long fecundated with patriot gore !

Flow on, thou genuine Hesperian blood,
And warm our bosoms with thy sacred flood,
That should grim Tyranny infest our plains
(Which Heaven avert!), full million patriot veins
May whelm her down, and prove not vainly won
Were Freedom's stars by godlike Washington!

NOTES.

WHEREVER in the poem a passage or expression is based on the authority of Bancroft or Irving, I have not considered it necessary to adduce their testimony, those brilliant and authentic writers being deservedly in the hands of everybody.

> Page 11.—*Hesperia's sons against Britannia's king*
> *For Freedom battling, Alleghania, sing!*

The word *America* cannot be easily handled in verse. Besides, it is considered by many writers an inappropriate term for our Republic. No poet could manage *The United States of America*. *Columbia* is old-fashioned, trite, and puerile. I have, therefore, chosen to call our country *Hesperia*, and our countrymen *Hesperians*. Hesperia means the Evening, *i.e.* the Western Land, and our Republic certainly deserves that name by excellence. It was the custom of the ancient poets to attribute the term to a great region lying farthest to the west. Thus Italy first received the appellation. Virgil: "Est locus, Hesperiam Graii cognomine dicunt." Æneid, I. 530. "Hesperia in magna." Id. vii. 4, et sæpe in eodem poemate. Afterwards it was applied to Spain, being still farther to the west. Horace uses it in this sense in his ode to Plotius Numida: "Qui nunc Hesperia sospes ab ultima." I. Od. 36, 4. Had our country been known then, it is very probable that these illustrious bards would have graced it with the title "Hesperia magna," in preference to all others. Even distinguished authors of the present day seem to incline to that expression. Thus Motley speaks of

America as "the great Western Republic." *R. D. R. I. 6.*
There exists, therefore, some ground for the poetic license I
have employed.

Alleghania, as a term for the Muse, was first suggested to me
by Irving's intimation to call our country *Alleghania* or *Appalachia.* So *Ontario* for the State, *Manhattan* for the City of New
York. See *Spanish Papers*, vol. ii.

The king of Britain is especially mentioned, because, as is
well known, our difficulties lay with him, not with Parliament
or with the nation.

> Page 23.—*Ontario's sons consigned the doubtful day*
> *To Clinton, Livingston, and youthful Jay.*

It will be seen that among the framers of Independence, as
named here, are given some who did not actually sign the declaration, but who, nevertheless, contributed more to it perhaps
than others who merely affixed their names.

> Page 38.—*Such was our hireling foe; in lustful Rall*
> *See every Hessian, and from one know all.*

These words must be a slender justification of the somewhat
repulsive portrait I have drawn of the Herr Colonel. He is intended for a type of what the Hessians generally were. But
though there exist perhaps no express authority for everything
fastened by me on the reckless foreigner, still I think that
nothing has been said against him which he did not richly
deserve.

> Page 44.—*Thayendanegea,* the Indian name of Joseph Brant.

> Page 48.— *Yet Crema, etc.*
Crema for the sadly-known Jane McCrea.

For the benefit of critics, I may as well remark here that, in
deference to caligraphy, I have not placed the mark of contraction in such words as *wanderer, beverage, heaven,* and the
like, though according to the metre they should generally be
read *wand'rer, bev'rage, heav'n,* etc.

Page 62.— *While bitter factions more than tyrant's love*
Her recreant minions to the combat move.

This is clearly shown by the conduct of the Tories in every
encounter with the patriots. In proof of which read the learned
Dawson's account of the Massacre at Wyoming, where the same
Johnsonian and Butleranian hordes signalized themselves in
their fiendish work. He says: "A patriot, named Henry Pensil,
while concealed among the willows on the margin of the river,
discovered his own brother approaching, and immediately came
forth, threw himself at his feet, begging for protection, and
promising to serve him for life if he would spare him. With a
look of contempt the heartless wretch replied: 'Mighty well,
you damned rebel,' and instantly shot him dead. Another,
Lieutenant Elijah Shoemaker, whose abundant means had long
enabled him to respond to the promptings of a charitable dis-
position in dispensing his bounty to the distressed, had also
sought refuge in the river. He was soon afterwards discovered
by a wretch named Windecker, whose troubles had frequently
been soothed by his unhappy victim; and with a 'Come out,
come out, you know I will protect you,' he invited him to leave
his hiding-place, and extended his left hand to assist him in
doing so. Before the victim reached the shore, however, Windecker dashed his hatchet into the head of his benefactor, who
fell back, and immediately floated away."—*Battles of the United
States.* Book I. chap. xxxviii.

Page 66.—*Thus grew my Stark,* etc.

This summary of Stark's early life is mainly taken from
Duyckinck's Biographies of Eminent Americans; art. John
Stark. See, also, Canto ix., for the same author's account of
sea-famed Jones.

Page 69.—*Thus Cincinnatus leaning on his spade,* etc.

Confer Livii Hist. Lib. III. Cap. 26.

Page 77.—*Truth, Hope, and Love inwreathed their fairest bay*
　　　　　Round him who saved his country by delay.

　　"Unus homo nobis cunctando restituit rem; .
　　Non ponebat enim rumores ante salutum;
　　Ergo postque magisque viri nunc gloria claret."—ENNIUS.

Page 87.—*Again thy fury waked in Brant's fierce soul.*

Most historians have attributed the chief part of the desola-
tion of Wyoming to the well-known brutality of Brant.　Some,
however, have labored to prove that he was not at all in that
vicinity at the time.　Others have even attempted to justify the
ignominious Butler of his sanguinary share.　This looks very
much like Byron's justification of Lucifer in his "Mystery of
Cain."　If Brant was not there in body, he was at least present
in soul; Giengwahtoh, or Gucingerachton, the actual leader of
the Indians at Wyoming, was nothing but the instrument of
Brant.　If Butler made a feeble attempt at mercy for the defenceless whites, was he not the avowed leader of those detest-
able Tories, whose greatest delight was to butcher their former
benefactors and even their genuine brothers?　John Butler's
name is infamous, and will remain so forever to every true
American heart.　Compare first note, preceding page.

Ibid.—*Fair Wyoming! thee threats the bloody storm,*
　　　　Thee brightly decked in Nature's fairest form.

For a description of this beautiful valley, see Peck's and
Miner's Wyoming, or quotations from them by Dawson in the
chapter cited above.

The stream alluded to in the subsequent lines is the Ohio.

Page 91.—*But Verplanck Abyla's less grandeur chose;*
　　　　　Like Calpe unsubdued high Rockpoint rose.

Abyla and Calpe, ancient names for the modern Ceuta and
Gibraltar.

Page 94.—*Before them stood the hope-forlorn.*

"The full of hope, misnamed 'forlorn,'
Who hold the thought of death in scorn,
And win their way with falchions' force,
Or pave the path with many a corse,
O'er which the following brave may rise,
Their stepping-stone—the last who dies!"
                      BYRON, Siege of Corinth, x.

Page 98.—*Thus now Minerva found her heavenly Sire
            Against foul Catherine breathing deadly ire.*

Catherine, the Russian empress or tigress, or whatever you like, provided it be sufficiently horrid; for kings and queens never mean anything else. That infamous woman's robbery of afflicted Poland, as well as her impious intermixture of God's sacred authority with whatever of despotism she undertook, and then her flagitious thanks to the Creator for the victory obtained over innocent fellow-creatures, are too notorious to be here repeated. Nor, alas! need we go back to Catherine for a knowledge of such impiety. As late as the beginning of this year have clouds of incense ascended to heaven in thanksgiving for the defeat of a patriot, whose pure desire was to see Rome again what it had been in the days of a Brutus and a Tully. When shall enlightened Liberty blot out these horrors, and give us an age that will worship God as the tender Father of all?

Page 103.—*Jones rigged his vessel vowed to Heaven's Maid
            With her own name.*

In this I have allowed myself a poetic license. The squadron commanded by Jones consisted of the Bon Homme Richard, his own ship, the Pallas, the Vengeance, the Alliance, and the Cerf. Between the Richard and the Serapis the main combat ensued; while the Pallas secured the capture of the Countess of Scarborough. Through the insubordination of Captain Landais, a whimsical Frenchman, the other three vessels were prevented from taking part in the conflict.

13

Page 104.—*Serapis*. Milton places the accent on the first syllable:

"Belus or Serapis, their gods."—Par. Lost, I.;

for which appear no authorities except Martianus Capella, Prudentius, and Paulinus Nolanus, all post-classical writers. Callimachus Epicus, a genuine Greek poet, has the penultimate long, and so it is fixed by all prosodists and lexicographers.

Page 118.—*Such later still the bold Batavians were,*
When patriot Haring all alone could dare
Fierce Alva's thousand on the Diemer-mound,
Till, safe his comrades all, he swam the blood-dyed sound.

"John Haring, of Horn, had planted himself entirely alone upon the dyke, where it was so narrow between the Y on the one side and the Diemer Lake on the other, that two men could hardly stand abreast. Here, armed with sword and shield, he had actually opposed and held in check one thousand of the enemy, during a period long enough to enable his own men, if they had been willing, to rally and effectually to repel the attack. It was too late, the battle was too far lost to be restored; but still the brave soldier held the post, till, by his devotion, he had enabled all those of his compatriots who still remained in the entrenchments to make good their retreat. He then plunged into the sea, and, untouched by spear or bullet, effected his escape. Had he been a Greek or a Roman, an Horatius or a Chabrias, his name would have been famous in history—his statue erected in the market-place; for the bold Dutchman on his dyke had manifested as much valor in a sacred cause as the most classic heroes of antiquity."—*Motley's Rise of the Dutch Republic*, vol. ii. p. 441.

The same daring Batavian shortly afterwards lost his life in a naval encounter on the Zuyder Zee. Fearlessly clambering on board the "Inquisition," and hauling down her colors, he was shot through the body and died on deck of the ship, which was not quite ready to strike her flag.—*Id. ibid.* p. 492.

Page 121.—*And as up Penn's steep cliff the iron horse*
Swift rushing yet exerts such equal force,
That in the night the rider scarce can know
He mounts a steep with yawning dells below.

So it seemed to me at least, when still a boy I crossed the
Alleghanies. It was for the first time, and I was naturally very
anxious to witness the ascent. When the train had reached
Allentown, I heard that the cliffs were before us. It was a dark,
tempestuous night. I almost strained my eyes out to see the
mountains as we hurried swiftly on. Nothing of a mountainous
character, however, appeared; nor did the cars seem to hang
in a different position than usual. Turning to a worthy gen-
tleman I asked whether we had yet reached the mountain.
" Why," said he, " we are near the top already." This vexed
me not a little; and I determined not to cross the Alleghanies
again in the night-time.

Page 128.—*Which gods bestow on every patriot brave,*
Th' Elysian fields.

Conf. Virg. "Hic manus, ob patriam pugnando vulnera
passi," et præcedentia.—*Æneid,* vi. 660.

Page 132.—*Tahlequah,* for the Indian Territory of which it is
the capital. It may be asked why I did not add Alaska to my
poetic list of States and Territories. The truth is that at the
time when this was written, very grave doubts existed in the
minds of my countrymen as to the propriety of our recent pur-
chases. Even the most enterprising individuals entertained a
holy horror for the ice-huts of Sitka no less than for the tottering headlands of Danish Thomas. When the huts of the former
shall have given place to stately or at least comfortable houses,
and the capes of the latter shall have ceased to shake, some
future and more gifted bard may supply the deficiency.

Page 134.—*He was so kind.*

Even the bitterest enemies of our Union-saving President must concede this. Foe and friend were alike to him, whenever there was question of bestowing a pardon or a favor. His misfortune was that, being placed in a time of faction, he could not please one party without offending the other. It is only after present prejudices have died out, that Lincoln can receive his due merit in the page of history and poetry.